CAUGHT IN TERROR

Terror begins for Barbara Young when she is kidnapped one evening on her way home from work. When she awakes from a drugged sleep she has, at first, no idea what her captors want. Terror mounts as the answer becomes clear, and, knowing that the men will kill her if they realise that she can't help them, Barbara begins a desperate bluff. Help comes unexpectedly when a ruthless killer strikes, but then, with the police net closing round them, the gang become more and more desperate . . .

Books by Michael Bardsley
in the Linford Mystery Library:

MURDER ON ICE
MURDER ON FIRE
MURDER FOR SALE
HIT IT RICH

MICHAEL BARDSLEY

◆

CAUGHT IN TERROR

Complete and Unabridged

LINFORD
Leicester

First published in Great Britain in 1969 by
Robert Hale Limited
London

First Linford Edition
published 2004
by arrangement with
Robert Hale Limited
London

British Library CIP Data

Bardsley, Michael
   Caught in terror.—Large print ed.—
Linford mystery library
   1. Kidnapping — Fiction
   2. Detective and mystery stories
   3. Large type books
   I. Title
   823.9′14 [F]

   ISBN 1–84395–318–8

Published by
F. A. Thorpe (Publishing)
Anstey, Leicestershire

Set by Words & Graphics Ltd.
Anstey, Leicestershire
Printed and bound in Great Britain by
T. J. International Ltd., Padstow, Cornwall

This book is printed on acid-free paper

1

Barbara Young walked quickly on her way home from work. There was always hurry to get home for tea, of course, but this evening there was even more hurry than normal. Two months ago, she had taken an exam in shorthand, and as the date for the results had drawn nearer she had been expecting them every day; that morning her mother had rung her up to tell her that there was a letter for her, marked with the college address on the envelope.

She had told her mother to leave it until she got home, so that she could open it herself.

If she passed, her boss had promised her another pound a week. She hurried, anxious to see the result, wondering what she could do with the pound if she had passed.

A whole pound a week extra.

She could put most of it towards new

clothes. Perhaps if she bought fewer sweets at lunchtime, and saved most of the pound, she could have a new dress every month. If he gave her the pound from this week, which he might as it was only Monday, she would be able to get that blue dress by Friday, the one with the white frill round the collar that she liked so much but which was too expensive for her at the moment.

She came to the road junction, and stopped, waiting to cross the road, jogging impatiently from one foot to the other as the stream of cars flowed past. She was tempted to run across and hope that she would make it without being knocked down, but natural caution held her back. In the midst of all the traffic she could see a cyclist, a small boy. He didn't look afraid, not even when two buses passed very close to him.

He caught sight of Barbara and waved.

She waved back, recognizing him as the boy she sometimes saw in the morning, delivering papers.

A gap came in the traffic.

She ran across the road, then slowed

down to a walk when she reached the opposite pavement. A boy of about her own age passed very near, turning his head to look at her as he drew level. Although she saw him, she pretended to ignore him; at nineteen, she had the face and figure to attract many boys, but she already had a boyfriend, and she was the type who believed in going out with just one boy at a time.

She walked for two blocks, and then turned off.

In the side street, the noise of the traffic dimmed suddenly and when she turned another corner it diminished even more, so that it was hard to imagine that there was so much traffic and so many people on the main road.

The street here only had houses on one side of it. On the other was a large playing field, nearly always crowded with children as in this part of London it was difficult to find somewhere to play. Even though it was half past five, and January, there was still enough light for her to see clearly across the field to the swings and roundabouts, and the see-saw with three small girls arguing which two of them should use it. Because it was cold, and so near tea-time, there were only these three, and a small boy there. The boy was lying on the ground, shooting at the girls with an imaginary machine gun.

When he saw Barbara he turned it on her.

Rat-tat-tat-tat.

She smiled, walking a little more slowly now, wondering whether to go home across the field or round by the road. It was longer to walk round by the road, but the playing field was likely to be a bit muddy after the rain that had fallen recently, and would spoil her shoes and stockings.

She decided to go by road.

Had she passed that exam?

A whole pound a week, and the blue dress, if she had. She pictured the dress as she walked, short, as she liked them, with white round the collar and hem, to set off her legs. Tim would like that, she thought. He was constantly telling her that she had good legs, and approved of anything that drew attention to them.

In front of her, a car came out of a side street.

Barbara took no notice of it, but as it drew level with her she saw the front dip, as if the driver had braked sharply. Still looking, she saw a woman lean out of the driver's window and beckon to her. Barbara stepped into the road. The car was very new, painted a shiny kind of blue, something like the dress; the woman seemed to be on her own, too, almost lost inside the large car.

'Can you tell me where Duncannon Road is?' the woman asked. 'All the roads round here look alike, and I seem to have got lost.'

Barbara moved nearer. The woman had spoken in so soft a voice that she could hardly make out the words. She raised her hand to point out a direction. As she did so, the rear door opened and a man climbed out. Swiftly and without a sound he wrapped great arms round Barbara, lifting her bodily into the back of the car. She tried to scream; a hand clamped over her mouth. She heard the door bang shut, and then felt the car picking up speed.

Sprawling on the seat, she realized that there were two men in the car. The one who had picked her up still had hold of her mouth and shoulders; the second one was lifting her legs from the seat. She tried to kick him as he silently unbuttoned her coat but he ignored the blows. Her struggles increased as he moved her coat to one side and pushed her dress up to her waist.

He took a syringe from the door pocket.

She swayed as the car took a corner; the man grunted softly and wedged her legs securely in the crook of one arm. His eyes narrowed as he bent towards her, then she felt the prick of the needle in the bare part of her thigh. She tried to scream as he pressed the plunger, but the other man's fingers were there, compressing her lips against her teeth, choking and hurting her. She felt the liquid in the syringe as it was forced into the vein, then her legs were released and she fell on to the cold leather of the seat.

The man grunted again, but she hardly heard him as the waves of sickness passed

6

over her. Then the sickness turned to blackness and she felt as if she were falling from a great height.

At the bottom of her fall, a pit of blackness opened to swallow her.

★　★　★

'Well, where is she?' Mildred Young asked helplessly.

'Probably quite simple.' Her husband grunted, tamping tobacco into his pipe with two fingers. He packed it in well, then struck a match. The breeze from the open window caught it and blew it out. 'Blast.' He lit another one, turning so that it burned fiercely. 'Probably she's met that Tim on the way home and she's stopped to talk to him. You know what girls are like at her age!'

The pipe was drawing well now, and he laughed as he threw the match into the fire and sat down.

'You ought to know, you were one yourself.'

'But doesn't it worry you?'

Mildred looked at her husband with

exasperation. Thirty-two years of marriage to him had still not altered the fact that she found his complete calmness, no matter what happened, irritating sometimes. Now, it made her feel as if she wanted to scream, as if she wanted to take hold of him and shake him until he was no longer calm.

She did nothing.

He reached over the side of the chair, to where the newspaper was lying on the floor, picked it up and straightened the pages. When he had finished, he laid it on his knee, as if he were going to read it.

If he did that, it would be too much.

He kept the paper on his knee without opening it.

'She'll have met that Tim,' he repeated, though with a little less conviction than he had had before.

'And how many times does she normally meet him on the way home from work?' demanded Mildred, her voice harsh. She glanced at the clock, on the mantelpiece over the fire. 'It's seven now. You know that she's normally home at quarter past six and that she'd be hurrying tonight anyway. You know that she wants those exam results.'

'That's probably it,' her husband grunted. 'She's afraid that she's failed and she doesn't want to come in and find out for sure.'

He was still calm. One hand rested on the paper, the other one played with the pipe, from which a thin spiral of smoke curled. At fifty-one, Harry Young was running to fat slightly, which he knew was due entirely to lack of exercise. Up to a couple of years ago he had been reasonably fit, but then he had been promoted to assistant manager at the firm of fur and skin dealers where he worked, and had got the new car that went with the position. He had never been able to afford a car before, although he had held a driving licence for many years, and the unaccustomed luxury had made him cut down on his walking to a great extent.

All he wanted now was to come home at nights to his paper and his wife, still pretty at forty-nine, and his daughter, who looked just as Millie had done when they were married.

Mildred stood with one hand by the clock. 'Don't be silly,' she said, her voice still shrill. 'She was looking forward to getting them. They were going to give her another pound a week if she'd passed. She was going to buy a lot of new dresses with it.'

'She won't get many for a pound,' Harry commented.

'Not all at once.' Millie was irritated, yet grateful because she sensed that he was joking to try to allay her fears that something had happened to Barbara. 'She was going to save it week by week.'

'Look, Millie,' Harry said, pulling his pipe out of his mouth and pointing it at her, 'you're panicking over nothing. She'll have met Tim and forgotten the time.'

He opened the paper.

'Harry!'

'What?'

'Put that paper down for a minute!' She reached over, almost snatching it from his hand. 'Can't you see that Barbara isn't here, and that she should have been here an hour ago?'

'That's it,' Harry Young agreed, sighing.

'She's only an hour late, Millie. That's hardly anything. If you really want to be sure, ring up Tim and ask him.'

'But I hardly know him!'

'Neither do I. I know where he lives, though. Do you want me to go round and see him?'

His wife hesitated now that she was confronted with definite action. Anxious as she was about Barbara, she was, as Harry had told her, only an hour late. She was nineteen, too, hardly a baby. If she hadn't come in another hour, that would be time enough to do something.

She tried to remember Tim's surname, but couldn't. It was something unusual, she was sure, but the name itself escaped her.

If Barbara had gone round there, wouldn't he have brought her back on his motor scooter? It wouldn't have taken him five minutes to slip round here. She looked at her husband, who had started on the paper.

Calm.

She wished that she could be as calm as he was, though probably she felt this

11

more, being Barbara's mother. Yet that shouldn't matter; as her father he should have just as much feeling.

She looked at the clock.

Barbara was well over an hour late now.

She looked back at Harry, sitting stoically in the chair reading and smoking his pipe. There must be some reason why he was taking no notice of Barbara's disappearance. Soon, he would have to do something.

If he cared.

2

It was fantastic.

Had her husband anything to do with Barbara's non-appearance? Why should he have? There was no way that she could think of in which he could be involved, and slowly reason began to take over again and the wild thoughts which had been going round her mind calmed slightly. It was natural that he should be like this, she thought. He was always so calm about everything; the time to start worrying was when he got worked up about things, when he ran around, shouting frantically.

She glanced round the room, her eyes falling on the envelope propped on the sideboard where they always left letters. It had been there all day, pale blue and thin, almost like the airmail letters that Barbara sometimes got from her American pen-friend. This was postmarked London, though, and was overstamped with the name of the college where she had taken the exam. Millie had wanted to open it as soon as it had come, before she had gone to phone Barbara, but she had resisted the temptation.

This was one of the reasons why Barbara should have hurried home.

The second one was that it was a Monday, the day on which she always stayed in and watched her favourite television programme. If she hurried she could get home and have her tea before the programme started, instead of having to eat it from a tray while she watched.

She would be too late now, anyway, Millie thought.

The television was new, too, something that they had only had since Harry's promotion. She had never realized before he got the new job how tight money had been, and how she had come to watch the spending automatically, so that they wouldn't go short when Friday came.

And Harry never would let her go to work.

After another glance at him she turned and left the room.

Barbara was at Tim's, she told herself.

★ ★ ★

At nine o'clock Barbara still hadn't returned.

★ ★ ★

Mildred Young was upstairs. She had been there, sitting in front of the dressing-table, since half past seven. It wasn't cold up here as they had a small electric fire which they used in the bedrooms to warm them up, and she had switched that on before sitting down. Gradually it had grown darker, until, almost without realizing it, she had been sitting there in the pitch dark.

She gave a funny little laugh.

By now, it was obvious that Barbara wasn't at Tim's.

There was no point in sitting here in the darkness, she told herself. She ought to get up and do something, even if it was only switching on the light. If she did that, she would have to draw the curtains, and then she would go and see what Harry had to suggest.

He would still be sitting there with the paper on his knee and his pipe sending up its curls of smoke. He would be so calm and, in her present mood, so irritating.

She stood up, smoothing down her dress, and crossed to the window. From here, you could normally see across the estate, as the road where their house was built was higher than the other roads, but now, with the darkness, Mildred could only see as far as the houses opposite. Most of them were curtained; in the one that wasn't she could see right into the lounge. Funny, she thought, how some people never bothered that anyone might see them accidentally, as she was doing now. She could see a girl, sitting on a chair, sprawling would be more the word, eating what looked like an apple and gazing at the television. She had a towel round her head as if she had just washed her hair.

That was how Barbara often sat.

Tears pricked at her eyes.

She turned away from the lighted

window, quickly, reaching up to the curtains. The ones in this room had always been hard to draw, even since they had put them up. Harry had always been going to alter the fittings, but it was one of the jobs he had never got round to, one of the things that he had never had time to do.

She pulled them quickly, then switched on the light.

She caught sight of herself in the mirror, and gasped.

Her face was drawn, her eyes red-rimmed as if she had been crying. Yet she hadn't. Her face, too, was white, not the funny sort of shade it went sometimes when she was feeling a little off-colour, but completely white, like a sheet of paper. A bright red spot stood out on each cheek, where she had put on some make-up before Harry had come home, but apart from that there was no colour.

She shook herself.

She couldn't go downstairs looking like that.

Or could she? If Harry saw her now, it might shake some of the calmness out of him, and she had the feeling that unless Harry did something, unless he showed in some way that he was bothered, either about her or about their daughter, her head would burst.

Their daughter.

Yet she was the only one making any fuss because she hadn't come home from work.

Work. The word seemed to strike some note in her head. Had she even left work? Perhaps they ought to try the office before they did anything else. She could recall one other occasion when something had come in unexpectedly, and Barbara had had to stay very late to get it finished. But on that occasion, Mildred remembered, she had sent a message, someone she worked with had called round.

This time, no one had called.

Not bothering about her appearance she ran down the stairs and burst into the room where her husband was sitting, still reading the paper.

Calm. So calm that she wanted to scream at him.

'Harry, what are we going to do?'

He looked up at her, and for a moment seemed startled. 'What have you been doing?'

'Worrying.' Wildly, Millie looked round. The envelope was still there, the fire was nearly out. She crossed to the old bucket that they used as a scuttle and shook some of the pieces out. Flames blazed and flickered. 'Worrying about where our daughter is, Harry. *Our* daughter.'

Harry Young stood up, dropping the paper dangerously near to the fire. He saw what he had done and kicked the sheets away. 'Why,' he said, 'you — you're as white as that paper.'

'That's right.' Millie was almost screaming. 'I'm as white as that paper that you've been sitting reading while I've been worrying about our daughter. Our daughter!' she repeated, her voice rising even higher.

Her husband put his arm round her shoulders. 'Now look, Millie, there's probably some simple explanation. You stay here and I'll go round to see Tim and see if she's there. That's probably where she is.'

He led Millie over to the chair and sat her down.

'Now don't you worry. I won't be very long, and then Barbara'll be back and everything will be all right.'

He went to the other room, where his coat was, laid over the back of an armchair, together with the cloth cap that he always liked to wear. He put them both on, made sure that the car keys were in the pocket then returned to where Millie was.

'I won't be very long.'

'Harry,' Millie almost whispered.

'Yes, love?'

'Do you think she could still be at work? You remember before — '

'I'll go round there too,' he promised. 'If she is there I'll have a word or two to say to that Little about it.'

His wife jerked up suddenly. 'Be careful what you say, Harry. You don't want to go losing her the job.'

'If it's that kind of a job, she's better off with it lost,' Harry said, and went out.

★ ★ ★

After her husband had gone out, Millie sat in the chair for a few minutes. She felt very tired, a feeling that she had never had before. Harry would be some time; half an hour at least, probably more. She decided to go upstairs and lie down for a bit; that would be better than just sitting here. She might even manage to sleep a little, too; that would be better still.

She stood up.

She felt an unfamiliar twinge in her chest, and gasped slightly.

The pain passed and she walked to the stairs, then climbed them slowly. Half-way up was a bend, and in it a frosted glass window that let some light into this dark part. Through it came the light of the street lamp outside, queerly bent and altered by the ripples on the glass, so that it was thrown all over the staircase in a dappled pattern.

She went on, into the bedroom, crossed to the window and twitched back the curtain, looking out, hoping to see Barbara.

A young man stood by the lamp post outside, not leaning on it, just standing near it, gazing insolently at the house, his hands in his pockets. Mildred watched him, but he didn't move, just stared back at her. His face showed up clearly in the light; she thought that he looked like a clown, with a queer round head and a wide mouth.

She let the curtain fall back, turned quickly and went to the bed.

The pain came again, sharper than before. This time, she cried out, it was so sharp and sudden.

A man was watching the house.

Why?

What did he want? Suddenly she wished that Harry were back to deal with this new crisis, and she wondered desperately what she should do. If he were still there when Harry came back, he could go out and ask him what he was doing, but what should she do if he tried to get in before that?

There was another significance, too.

The man must be connected in some way with Barbara's disappearance. That meant that she couldn't be either at work or at Tim's flat.

Millie shut her eyes and lay on the bed, wincing with the pain that seemed to grow sharper every time she breathed.

★ ★ ★

Harry Young left his car outside the small block of flats where he knew Tim Bocking lived and walked quickly to the entrance. He had never been inside the block before, although he had passed it often enough; once through the door he stopped, uncertain what to do next, then saw a board fastened to the wall. There was a list of five flat numbers on it, with a name opposite each. Tim's name was against number three.

Harry went quickly up the stairs.

Flats one and two were on the ground floor, together with some shops that faced on to the street. Above these were the rest of the flats, opening off a narrow corridor. As Harry stepped off the landing into the passage, he saw a girl further along, near where he judged Bocking's door would be. She had one hand raised to the bell, obviously calling at the flat. Harry walked slowly, until he reached the door. The young woman had received no answer to her ring, and as Harry came up she turned.

She was a little older than Barbara, he thought, although the eye shadow and make-up that she wore made it difficult to judge her age. Her hair was long, and tucked inside the collar of the fur coat that she wore; a coat that Harry's expert eye recognized as one that was quite expensive.

When she spoke it was in an unexpectedly firm and sure voice.

'Are you looking for Tim Bocking, too?' she asked.

Harry nodded.

'I don't think he's in. I've been ringing here for nearly five minutes and there isn't an answer.'

'Are you sure the bell works?' Harry asked.

The girl laughed. 'I've knocked, too. In fact, I've made so much noise that I'm surprised everyone else hasn't heard me, too.'

Harry pursed his lips. If Bocking wasn't

in there was nothing else he could do here. He smiled at the girl, told her that there was no point in staying here and walked with her to the entrance. She left him there, walking off in the opposite direction to which he would go.

As yet, there was no reason to connect her with what had happened to Barbara.

★ ★ ★

Mildred Young heard the sound of the key in the lock, and started up quickly. This must be Harry back already.

She called to him.

'Where are you?' he shouted back.

'Here, upstairs.' Her voice was faint, and her throat hurt as if she wanted a drink. She heard Harry shut the door, heard the sound of his feet on the stairs and then he came into the room.

'Are you all right?' he asked, bending over her.

'I — yes. Harry!'

'Yes, love?'

Still the same calmness about him.

Panic rose in her breast as she remembered the man outside. She told Harry about him. 'Did you see him when you came in?' she finished, looking at him anxiously, pleading almost, that he would offer some clue as to where Barbara was.

'Man? What man?'

'By the lamp!' Her voice rose until it was a shrill scream. 'By the lamp, a man watching the house!' She slid off the bed, her breath rasping, and went over to the window.

There was no one in the street.

'There wasn't anyone there when I came in, either,' Harry said. 'You're imagining things, love.'

'I'm not! I'm not! I — ' She broke off. 'Was Barbara there?'

He shook his head. 'She wasn't at the flat. There was another woman looking for Tim, but there was no answer at the door.'

'Another woman? What sort of woman?'

Patiently, Harry told her. 'I rang Lennon's too,' he finished. 'There was no answer, so I suppose she wasn't there.'

Millie stared at him, her mouth open

slightly, the pain still nagging in her chest. Suddenly she put both hands to her head.

'Oh, God, Harry, what are we going to do?'

Harry said nothing.

Mildred looked at him. He's there, she thought, calm, always calm. Suddenly the pain in her chest flared again, and a second pain started at the top of her head and seemed to engulf her whole body. She gasped and staggered a little. She saw Harry start forward, heard a scream but didn't know that she had made it, and staggered again.

Harry Young saw his wife collapse on the floor.

3

Maurice Franklin had been the Young's family doctor for nearly twenty years. When he had first moved to the Risely district of London he had been very young, only twenty-five, absurdly young in those days to be starting his own practice. A legacy had allowed him to do that; he had bought the practice, determined to get away from the depressing atmosphere of the hospital where he worked. He loved his work as a doctor, but not the way in which the hospital seniors ordered him around, and gave him all the worst cases to work on.

Ever since he had left medical school he had wanted his own practice.

He had got it, then, and had screwed the brass plate to the wall himself, polishing it proudly for those first few months when he couldn't afford a cleaner.

He had been a good doctor, and the

practice had prospered, until there was almost too much work. He had been tempted to take on a partner, but had always resisted, always afraid that if he did it would turn out like the hospital again, with him doing all the work and others taking all the credit.

Because of this, he had never had much leisure, never had much time to go out and meet people who weren't ill. He had never married.

He still had the same practice, although a lot of the patients had changed now.

The Young's hadn't.

They were just the same as he had always known them, though much older. They had been married for twelve years when he had taken over the practice, and had been childless then, though he had heard of a child, very early in the marriage, which had died not long after it had been born. Harry Young he knew as a solid, calm man, big, hefty, a bull of a man, but without the bull's temper; his wife was the one for that, pretty little Mildred, who looked so much like the daughter that

Franklin had helped to deliver.

He was surprised to get a phone call from Harry that night.

Harry sounded almost excited.

His wife, he said, had collapsed.

'I'll be right across,' Franklin promised, hanging up the phone and crossing to the door. Although he had no wife he did have a housekeeper, an old shrew of a woman who had been with him for fifteen years and who lived in a flat made from two of the upstairs rooms in the rambling old house where he lived. She had a nephew, her only relative, who was a junior doctor at one of the London hospitals; she didn't know it, but in his will Franklin had left the practice to him.

He opened the stairs door.

'Lil,' he called.

'All right, doctor.'

There was no bell or anything like that. His natural dislike of authority made him reluctant to impose it on others, and now he shouted up the stairs to his house-keeper, almost as if she were his wife, not a servant to be brought running at the ring of a bell. Every day after evening surgery, she would bring him his tea, and leave supper set out in the kitchen. He would eat the tea, leave the things in the kitchen to be washed in the morning and pick up the supper when he was ready for it. That way, she had every evening free, and he wasn't tied to set times for supper.

When he had to go out on a call he always shouted up the stairs like this.

His bag was ready packed in the hall. He picked it up and went out, slamming the door after him. The car was in the garage; he always put it away when he had made his last official call for the day, so that there was no danger of it being damaged. The garage was big and roomy, and as there was room in the house for anything that he wanted to store there was none of the junk in it that characterized most garages, so that it was easy to get the car out in a hurry.

He backed swiftly down the drive now, hearing the gravel scrunching under the tyres.

He paused briefly at the gates, until he was certain that there was nothing coming then reversed into the road and drove off. The garage doors would stay open; it was well hidden from the road by some tall trees, and there was nothing in it to steal.

Besides, there wasn't time to go back and shut them . . .

He drove fast but safely, wishing at times that he had some kind of lamp on his car to enable him to get through the traffic quickly. It was surprising how many cars were about, he thought. Didn't seem much when you were driving normally, but when you were in a hurry like this, every dawdling car held you up.

He wondered what could be wrong with Mildred Young. She had no history of illness, in fact she hadn't been to see him for almost a year, not since she had ricked her ankle the previous winter. From what her husband had said on the phone it sounded as if she had had a fit of some kind, but surely that wasn't possible.

There was nothing that could cause that.

Or was there?

Worry could do it, of course, and she

was a worrier. He must find out if she had had excess worry or strain lately; if she had, she could be in danger unless the pressure were removed quickly.

He reached the Young's house only ten minutes after Harry had phoned him.

He pulled up in the badly lit road, leaving all his car lights on and the keys in the dash, grabbed the bag from the seat beside him and hurried into the house.

Harry opened the door almost as his finger touched the bell.

'Where is she, Mr. Young?'

'In here, doctor.' Young took him into the front room where he had laid his wife on the big couch that stood along one wall, and covered her with a sheet, which seemed to emphasize the whiteness of her face.

Franklin drew breath with a little suck of sound.

'How long has she been like that?'

'About quarter of an hour.'

Franklin laid down his bag, opened it quickly and took out his instruments. He unfastened the high necked blouse and put one end of the stethoscope on the woman's chest. This was done almost automatically; all the time he was doing it he was thinking of something else, trying to pin down what was wrong, what was nagging at the back of his mind.

He looked up at Young.

'Can you nip out and phone for an ambulance?'

'What's the matter?' Young was almost whispering.

'Don't argue man, get that ambulance!'

Young hurried out. While he was gone the doctor busied himself with the woman. All the time, she lay still, so still that she might have been dead.

The only colour in her face was the faint tinge of blue around her lips.

★ ★ ★

The ambulance arrived ten minutes later.

The odd thing was still nagging at Franklin's mind, but now he knew what it was. After he had supervised the loading of the woman into the back of the ambulance he turned to the driver.

'You know what to do. I'll follow later,

I've got one or two things to clear up here.'

'Okay, doctor.'

The driver hurried round to the cab. Seconds later he started the engine and the vehicle moved off, the flashing lamp seeming very bright in this dark road. Franklin thought he saw a curtain twitch at one of the houses across the road, but he ignored it.

He knew now what was wrong.

Harry Young, this calm, bull of a man, had been almost panicking about his wife.

Almost as if he thought that he was responsible for what had happened.

The two men went back into the house, and Franklin sat Young down in one of the easy chairs.

'Do you want to go with your wife, Mr. Young?'

'Would — would there be any point?'

'Not immediately. In fact, you'd probably only get in the way. They'll do what's needed at the hospital and let you know the minute that there's any change or anything that you can do.' Franklin gave him a reassuring smile.

'Which hospital's that? And what's wrong with her, doctor, what have I done?'

What have *I* done . . . ?

'She'll be at St. Thomas's for the moment,' Franklin answered. 'I think that she's had a mild stroke, but there's no need to worry about it. Suppose you tell me what happened.'

'She — she collapsed.'

'What happened before that? Was she worried about something?'

'Yes.'

'What?' Franklin spoke gently. If Young thought that it was his fault that his wife had collapsed there was no need to upset him further.

'Our Barbara's disappeared.'

Slowly, the story came out, how Mildred had been worried, how he, Harry, trying not to make her more worried had passed it off, of how he must have driven her almost mad by seeming that he couldn't care less about it.

'And then — that happened,' he finished. 'She just collapsed before my eyes.'

Franklin looked at him gravely. 'Have

36

you told the police about this?'

'Not yet. I did think that she might be with her boyfriend, but he's vanished too.'

Franklin stood up. 'I should think that it's very likely that they've gone somewhere together,' he commented. 'Go to the police and tell them exactly what's happened. Even if it turns out to be a false alarm, they won't mind. I'm going down to the hospital; the minute that I think you can do any good by being there, I'll let you know.'

After a few more words he left the house, hurrying slightly. It would probably do more harm than good to have Young at the hospital now, he thought. If his wife saw him like that she would start worrying all over again, this time about her husband.

He frowned. Bad of the girl to go off like that, of course. She might have given them some warning, but then, children never thought about things like that. Young love, of course, probably some opposition to the boyfriend from her parents.

He reached his car.

If she didn't return soon, it might kill her mother.

He fumbled in his pocket for the car keys, then remembered that he had left them in the dashboard, and that the car was still unlocked. He got in, sliding behind the wheel, starting the engine with one hand while shutting the door with the other.

He heard a faint sound of movement from the back seat, and turned.

Before he had time to turn round properly he felt something cold and hard pressing into the back of his neck. A voice said: 'Don't panic, doctor. Just do as you're told.'

4

Franklin's tongue flickered over his lips.
'Don't panic, doctor, just do as you're
told.' The words seemed to hang in his
mind. How often had he said something
like that to people in his surgery, or in
their own home when they had called him
in? How often had he wished that he had
some way of making sure that they didn't
panic, that they did everything that they
were told?

And now it was being said to him.

And there was the coldness of the gun
to back it up.

He said: 'What do you want?'

'Just drive off, doctor. Turn left at the
end of the street.'

Franklin let in the clutch and the car
moved off with a jerk. The cold circle at
his neck moved slightly and then pressed
harder.

'Don't try to be clever, doctor.'

'I'm not trying to be clever, damn you.

I'm trying to behave normally under abnormal conditions.'

'Dig that.' The voice spoke coldly and impersonally, as if it couldn't care less about Maurice Franklin or what he did, so long as it was what he was told to do.

He reached the end of the street and turned left.

'You know Mainford Road?' the voice asked.

'Yes.'

'Drive to it. Turn right at the Market Hall when you come to it, and stop.'

Franklin drove slowly, wondering if there was any way he could get this maniac out of his car and safely in the hands of the police. Obviously, he was having him drive somewhere quiet where he could either rob him or shoot him, or both.

The obvious escaped Franklin at that moment. He was too bothered with trying to get rid of the man to notice things.

'Where are we going?' he asked. If he knew that he might be able to work out a means of contacting the police on the way.

'Just be quiet, doctor, and do as you're told.'

It hit him then. The maniac knew that he was a doctor.

'How — ' he began, and then compressed his lips. Do as you're told, doctor. Don't ask questions. He reached the turning at Mainford Road, and paused to let a bus come past before making the turning. He turned right again at the Market Hall, having to wait longer this time, so long that he thought that he would never make the turn.

When he was round the corner he pulled into the side of the road.

'Leave the engine running, doctor.'

He started to turn his head again, to look into the back seat.

'Don't look round. Keep your eyes to the front. Have you all your gear with you?'

'What gear?'

'Your medico stuff.'

'What do you want me to do?' Impatience rose in Franklin.

'I want you to examine someone, doctor. Have you enough gear for that?'

41

'I have. What kind of an examination do you want me to do?'

'If I knew that I wouldn't need a doctor, would I?' The voice was still calm and impersonal. 'You have the things with you that you would take on any other case?'

'Yes.'

'Then you won't need to go back to your surgery for anything, will you?'

Again Franklin licked his lips, realizing that his last hope of rescue had been taken from him. He could say that he had suddenly remembered something important which he had left behind, but he doubted now if he would be believed.

'Will you?' the voice repeated, digging the gun into his neck.

'No,' Franklin answered carefully. 'There's no need to go back to the surgery.' He spoke as he might to a specialist who was known to be a bit of a tartar with GP's.

'Then drive on, doctor. Take the fourth turning on the left.'

Just like a driving test, Franklin thought, as he let in the clutch and moved off. Always doctor, never his name. That meant the only way in which this maniac knew that he was a doctor was from the ambulance outside the Young's house, that he must want a doctor for something illegal, and had either been passing or watching the Young's place, seen Franklin come, and selected him.

'Turn next right,' ordered the voice. 'And don't think so much, doctor.'

Franklin turned right, this time with a clear road. He trod heavily on the accelerator as he did so; the tyres squealed and the cold circle of the gun moved again as the maniac was thrown across the seat.

'Be careful, doctor.' The voice was slightly breathless. 'I could have had a finger on the trigger then. You don't want people looking at you, do you?'

Franklin made no answer, changing gear as smoothly as he could. His hands were very cold, and unsteady, yet when he looked down at the gear lever he could see the marks of his fingers clearly, as if he had been perspiring a lot.

Where were they going?

There was no point in trying to guess.

'Turn left and second right.'

He didn't know this part of London all that well, as he was now well out of the area covered by his practice. He knew that Maida Vale was somewhere on his left, but beyond that he was lost. He drove slowly, trying to make out something that would show him exactly where he was, but the road was very dark. On either side of it, trees rose up, as if it were in one of the better class suburbs, but they weren't usually so badly lit. He peered from side to side.

'Concentrate on the road, doctor. You don't want to have an accident, do you?' The voice chuckled slightly, putting a horrible emphasis on the word 'accident'.

Franklin speeded up a little, unsure whether or not the man would actually kill him. He thought not, because he wanted a doctor, but on the other hand he seemed slightly mad, and there was no telling what someone in that state of mind would do.

'Turn left and then third right.'

Franklin turned left. As he did so he saw a car coming towards him slowly.

A police car.

All he had to do was to make the turn a little shallower, so that he drifted across the road, towards the police car, blocking its path. The driver would be certain to make him stop, if only to make sure that he wasn't drunk, and that would sort out the maniac.

The voice in the back said: 'I'm still here, doctor. Don't get any smart ideas about the cop car. I can pull this trigger quicker than the cops can run.'

'I'm sure you can.' Franklin was almost opposite the police car now; by glancing across he could see the policeman driving it, his eyes fixed on the road ahead, taking no notice of Franklin's Riley.

The two cars passed.

Franklin drove on. He took the turning that the voice had indicated and found himself running on a much rougher surface; cobblestones, it seemed.

Almost as soon as he had made the turn the man told him to stop.

He stopped.

'Get out, doctor. Slowly, so that I can

see what you're doing. And don't forget your bag.'

Franklin picked up the bag and got out, slamming the car door. He heard the passenger door shut, and knew that the maniac was just behind him. He made no attempt to turn or to move, just stood by the bonnet of the car, awaiting instructions.

The man said: 'You're doing well. Now walk along a little and go up the steps of number twenty.'

Franklin walked, conscious of the nearness of the man and the gun. He glanced to one side, saw the number twenty on a gate and stopped, fumbling for the catch.

He climbed three stone steps.

'Press the bell.'

He pressed. After a few moments the door was opened by someone who stood behind it so that he couldn't be seen. The man who had been in the car pushed Franklin, so that he stumbled into the house.

He was in a passage; almost at his left hand a door opened off, another one was further along, with a third one at the end, towards which he was pushed. He opened it and went down a short flight of steps into a cellar. There was a light on, as if the cellar was in constant use, and there was no musty smell or cold feeling as there was in most cellars.

He stopped at the bottom of the steps, and one of the men pushed past him and stood in front of him.

'Be very careful, doctor. Do just what you're told.'

It was the man from the car. He was about the same height as the doctor, with hardly any hair on his head, and a round, moon face. The baldness in someone who was obviously only young surprised Franklin, but there was no time to speculate on it now.

'Come on in, doctor, your patient is in here.' The bald man led Franklin forward, round a stone pillar jutting out from the wall, past a heap of coal and a stack of chopped wood, into another room. When they entered this second room, the man stopped, turning and grinning, and Franklin thought that if he put on a mask and make-up he would look just like a clown. They went on, into the other half of the cellar, where a bed had been made up beneath a single unshaded bulb.

Someone lay on the bed, covered by a sheet.

Followed by the two men, Franklin went to the bed and laid his bag on the floor, just as he had done at the Young's house.

The person he had been brought here to examine was their daughter, Barbara, lying very still, looking very like her mother.

Even to the blue tinged lips.

5

All thought of his own danger was gone as Franklin stepped forward and turned down the sheet which covered Barbara. She was fully dressed beneath it, except for her coat, which lay on the floor at the foot of the bed, a muddy footprint on it where one of the men had walked across it. Working quickly, he unbuttoned the white cardigan she wore and eased it off her arms, then he stooped to his bag and took out thermometer and stethoscope. He popped the thermometer into the girl's slack mouth, then passed one hand beneath her shoulders.

Suddenly, he remembered where he was, and turned.

'I'd prefer to do this in private.'

'Can it, doctor,' the clown man said shortly. 'Just get on with it.'

Franklin shrugged, then gently unzipped the green linen dress and pulled it away from her shoulders, deliberately standing so that he hid her from the men. He pressed the stethoscope against her chest, listened to the weak heartbeat for a few moments, then took out the thermometer.

Barbara's temperature was abnormally low.

He said: 'She's been drugged.'

The clown man didn't speak. Franklin pulled the dress back into place, fastened it up and turned to the men.

'That's right,' the clown man said. 'We gave her too much. She should have recovered about an hour ago but she's shown no signs yet.'

There was just the faintest edge of panic to his voice, almost as if he were afraid that he had killed the girl, and he didn't want that.

Franklin asked: 'What is the drug?'

The man told him, passing him a crumpled packet and a syringe. Franklin took them, read the packet then took some white tablets out of his bag.

'Water?' he asked.

'Hot or cold?' This time it wasn't the clown man who spoke but the other one, a much bigger man with an American accent.

'Cold.'

The man went out.

'And hurry,' Franklin called after him.

In a remarkably short time the man shambled back, carrying a bowl of water and a cup. Franklin nodded his thanks, filling the cup carefully. When he considered he had enough water in it he dropped in three of the tablets and watched them dissolve quickly, turning the water a milky white. When they had completely dissolved he took a fresh syringe from his case, drew some of the liquid into it and took hold of Barbara's forearm.

'It's a little crude,' he said, 'and I'd rather have taken her to my surgery where there are proper facilities, but I don't suppose you'd have allowed that, would you?'

'Just bring her round, doctor.'

A thin film of perspiration beaded Franklin's forehead as he jabbed the syringe home and pressed the plunger. When he withdrew it, he squeezed the rest of the liquid into the cup, then washed the syringe in the bowl.

'What happens now?' asked the clown man.

Franklin replaced the syringe in his case then picked up Barbara's cardigan and draped it round her shoulders and over her bare arms.

'We wait for about half an hour,' he said. 'At the end of that time I examine her again. If she's going to come round she'll be warmer and her heart beat will be stronger.'

He straightened up, walked round the bed and picked up the coat, pale blue, with a black collar. After shaking it to get rid of the dried mud of the footprint he put it on the bed as another blanket, making sure that it was fully over the girl.

All the time the two men watched him.

'What if nothing happens after half an hour?' the American asked.

'If nothing has happened,' Franklin answered, 'I very much doubt if she will come round at all.'

He looked very tired and old as he spoke.

* * *

At that moment, Harry Young was hanging up the phone after speaking to the police. They had listened to what he had to say, and had promised to send someone round to the house to take full particulars.

He, too, looked very old and tired.

* * *

Half an hour later the clown man said: 'Doctor, she isn't moving.'

'She doesn't have to move,' Franklin replied irritably. 'Let me see her.'

The stethoscope was still hanging round his neck. He hooked the ends into his ears, flicked the thermometer to zero and stepped across to the girl to carry out his examination again. At the end of it he looked at the men and nodded.

'She's improving rapidly.'

'Is it certain that she'll come round?'

'Ninety per cent. Give her another half hour.'

The clown man nodded, looking at his companion.

Franklin said: 'And now will you tell me what this is all about?'

'No, doctor. You've been told all you need to know. The girl was drugged too heavily and we needed a doctor to bring her round. There was a slight error in the dose.'

'A slight error!' Franklin said, his eyebrows rising. 'If I made errors like that — ' He broke off. 'Why should you need to drug her in the first place?'

'Perhaps she was like you and asked too many questions.'

Franklin compressed his lips. He was afraid of these men, but there was no point in showing it; he might even make things worse for himself if he did. 'I must ask you again what she's doing here and what you're going to do with her when she comes round.'

'That's our business, doc. You don't ask all your patients what they're going to do when they're better, do you?'

'I don't see all my patients in cellars with gunmen standing by.'

'No.' The clown man nodded in agreement. 'Would you have come so quickly if we hadn't brought you like this?'

'Naturally. She's one of my patients. You must know that or you wouldn't have chosen me.'

The American spoke. 'You weren't chosen, doc, you chose yourself.'

'What do you mean?'

'I was watching the Young's house,' the clown man said. 'I knew we wanted a doctor and you happened to come along. Your hard luck, really.'

Franklin said nothing, just stared at the two men.

Eventually the clown man said: 'We don't want you to ask any more questions, doctor.'

'I can see that.'

'Then why don't you shut it,' snarled the American suddenly, coming very close to Franklin. 'Why don't you mind your own business and do as you're told?'

Franklin backed a pace; the American reached out and would have seized him if the other man hadn't held him back.

'Leave him for now, Tex. We need him for the girl.'

The man called Tex glared, first at the clown man and then at the doctor. For a moment Franklin thought that he was going to ignore the other's request, but he lowered his hand slowly, then turned and walked over to the girl.

'She's improving,' he observed. 'I can see her breathing. I couldn't before.'

Franklin pushed him to one side. 'Let me see.' The stethoscope was out again, dabbing at Barbara's chest. When he had finished he looked up at the men.

'Right, gentlemen,' he announced softly, 'she'll be all right now.'

'Are you sure?' the clown man asked.

'Positive.'

The clown man smiled. 'Oke, Tex,' he said.

Franklin swung round sharply, to where the American stood with a gun. He saw the expression on his face, saw the gun move and jerked up his arm in a feeble attempt to save himself.

Tex fired once.

Harry Young was in bed now. The police had sent a man round, who had listened carefully to his story and taken down all the relevant details. He had only been a young man, too young, Harry thought, to appreciate properly what he was doing, but he seemed to know the drill. After taking details of Barbara's usual habits he had asked for a recent photo of her, and some information about Tim Bocking. He had had a faint smile on his face when he had asked that; Harry was sure that he thought they had gone away together.

After twenty minutes, the policeman had left, promising him that they would do their best to find Barbara.

'If you hear anything yourself, sir, be sure to get in touch with us at once, won't you?'

Harry said he would. As soon as the man had left he went up to bed.

Poor Millie.

It was all his fault, too. If only he had taken more notice of her when she had told him about Barbara, and discussed it with her, she wouldn't have gone running off upstairs on her own. She must have been sitting there worrying all the time, while he had thought that she was reading a book and that she had gone up there to get out of the smoky atmosphere of the downstairs room, as she so often did. She didn't smoke, and she didn't like it very much when he did, even now, after thirty-two years.

Thirty-two years.

If anything happened to her he wouldn't know what to do. If anything happened to Barbara he wouldn't know what to do, either.

He dozed, but didn't sleep.

★ ★ ★

Not far away, in the house to which Maurice Franklin had been taken by a roundabout route, and in which he had died, Barbara Young lay on the bed. She was still unconscious, but her breathing was stronger now and it was obvious that she was recovering quickly from the drug.

Occasionally, she stirred slightly.

* ★ ★

In one of the rooms above her the two men sat in easy chairs, the clown man reading a paper-backed book and the American, Tex, just staring into the fire. After a while he got up and went down into the cellar, to look at the girl. When he got back upstairs he said:

'I guess it won't be long now.'

'Give her another couple of hours yet.'

'Why?' The American sat down in front of the fire again.

'It'll do her no harm to wonder where she is. She can't get out, can she?'

'Nope.' Tex shook his head. 'I don't think even I could get out of that cellar when it's locked.'

The clown man licked his lips.

'Good,' he said in his dry, precise voice, so unlike that of a clown. 'When she's ready, we'll get to work on her properly.'

59

6

Half an hour after the clown man had spoken, Barbara came round. She lay for some time with her eyes shut, feeling pleasantly drowsy, certain that she was in bed at home and that it wasn't time to get up yet. She moved one arm, felt something stab and hurt, and gasped.

Cautiously she moved again.

This time there was no pain. Reassured slightly she snuggled under the blanket more comfortably and opened her eyes. The light from the single bulb glared down painfully.

She shut them quickly.

After a few moments she tried again, slowly and cautiously, twisting her head so that the light didn't strike directly, and looking round. She didn't know where she was. She struggled to sit up, her arm pricking again, though not as painfully as it had done before and her cardigan sliding down where it was only draped round her shoulders.

Of course.

She remembered now.

The woman in the car. The man who had sprung out and grabbed her. The way they had held her and pushed her dress back and jabbed the syringe into her leg. She felt at her leg, pressing to see if it was painful where he had injected the drug, but she could feel nothing. Pulling her cardigan on properly, she pushed the bedclothes back and swung her legs over the side of the bed. Except for her coat and shoes she was fully dressed. She sat on the edge of the bed for a moment, feeling sick and dizzy, then stood up. The room whirled until she thought she was going to collapse but by leaning heavily on the bed and shutting her eyes she was able to make the feeling go away. As soon as she was better she was aware of the chill from the stone floor striking through to her bare feet.

She took a step forward.

Her shoes were on the floor by the bed; her coat she noticed at the foot, as if it had been used as a blanket.

She stooped and slipped her shoes on.

The door was in one corner of the room.

It would be locked, of course. Whoever had taken such trouble to get her here wouldn't let her escape so easily. She crossed to it, avoiding the electric fire in the middle of the floor, and turned the handle. It was locked; curiously, she felt no disappointment at this, probably because she had been expecting it so much. After tugging at it again, just to make sure, she turned back to the cellar. There was no window in this part of it, but half-way along one of the walls a pillar jutted out, whitewashed like every- thing else, cutting the cellar into two rooms and making what looked like a narrow passage.

She crossed to the pillar.

There was a passage, but no door or window. A small heap of coal lay near the pillar, some firewood just beyond it, and at the end of the passage a grating, set in the ceiling. By standing beneath this and looking up she could make out the holes in it, but they were too small for her to see through. When she reached up she found that even by standing on her toes she couldn't get to within a foot of it; there was no chance of pushing it up and getting out that way.

Unless . . .

Unless she could get the coal into a pile, and some of the firewood, too, and make a kind of platform. The difficulty, she saw at once, would be in making it strong enough to carry her weight. She didn't know, either, how long she would be undisturbed, or how much noise she could make without being overheard. Obviously there was no point in shouting for help; that would only bring her captors, who would either drug her again or tie her up. She shuddered; lying there helplessly bound would be worse, far worse, than lying unconscious and oblivious under drugs.

Who were her captors, anyway, and why had she been brought here?

She could see no answer to the question; the only thing to do was to put it out of her mind and concentrate on getting out.

She felt dizzy again, from the effects of the drug, and only just managed to get back to the bed before she collapsed. This was awful. She couldn't stand up for long enough to see if she could escape.

Why had she been brought here?

Much as she tried to put the question to the back of her mind she found it returning. There was no reason, as far as she could see. She was just a normal girl, there was nothing special about her that would make her a good subject for a kidnapping. Her parents hadn't a great deal of money, and certainly couldn't afford to pay a worthwhile ransom for her, so that motive was out.

She stared round at the grubby, white-washed walls.

What would be happening at home, now?

She still had on her wrist watch, and knew that the time was half-past ten. By now, it would be obvious that she wouldn't be coming home from work, and her parents would long ago have begun to wonder where she was. Her father, she knew, would be very calm about it, but her mother would panic.

Eventually they would go to the police.

She couldn't think beyond that.

Her mind went back to the people who had kidnapped her, to the woman in the shiny blue car.

The blue that had been so like the blue of the dress she was going to buy.

She stood up again and went back to the grating, which could be a way of escape if only she could get up to it and lever off the metal cover. Kneeling on the flag floor she managed to scrape together some bits of coal. Some of them were quite big lumps; these she laid on the floor itself to give a firm foundation. There weren't many, only enough to make a pile about a foot square. On top of this she made a criss-cross pattern with some of the sticks of wood, then stood up. Her hands were dirty from messing about with the coal; she banged them together and the surplus dust flew off in tiny clouds, making her cough when it got into her throat.

Gingerly, she put one foot on to the

platform, then gradually transferred all her weight to it.

It didn't collapse.

She brought up the other foot, then reached up. To her disappointment her groping fingers still fell short of the cover; stepping away from the platform she looked around for more coal. There didn't seem to be any; in fact all the bits she could see looked as if they had been deliberately chopped up into small pieces.

Her eye caught something else.

A stain on the floor.

She swallowed and walked over to it. It was adjoining the pillar, and there was half in one of the rooms, half in the other, which made her wonder why she hadn't seen it before. It was big enough not to be missed easily, irregular in shape and shone in the harsh glow of the light.

It shone so much that it looked sticky.

Slowly she bent to it, lightly dabbing one of her fingers at it. It was sticky. She withdrew the finger quickly and looked at it.

Only then did she realize that the stain was blood.

Only then did it occur to her that the people who had brought her here might intend to kill her.

Feeling faint and sick again she went back to the bed. There was no point in hurrying to get away, as the bits of wood and coal that remained wouldn't lift her so that she could reach the cover, and besides she felt that if she didn't have a short rest she would collapse again.

Suppose she had been brought here by a maniac?

Suppose that she was kept here for days, or even weeks, until he tired of her and killed her?

She shuddered, and then a comforting thought came. In the car that had kidnapped her there had been a woman driving, and surely a woman wouldn't be a party to anything like that? And if the maniac were friendly enough with one woman to get her to do things like that, why should he want another one?

What would the police do when her mother and father went to them?

They wouldn't know where to start looking for her. There were no clues, no one had seen her get into the blue car and there was nothing to connect her with the occupants. They would go to see Tim, of course, but he was away. The natural assumption would be that they had run away together, of course; that might throw everyone on the wrong track for days.

Tears pricked at the back of her eyes as she realized that there would be no help for many days, if at all.

If she was to get out, it would only be by her own efforts.

Slowly she stood up again. If only she didn't feel so dazed, so sick. This was the effect of the drug, and it needed a great effort to fight the desire to lie down and go back to sleep. Despairingly she looked at the coal and wood. There was no hope of making any kind of platform with them, as she had hoped. All the bits were too small, and even if she could make a platform out of them she doubted if it would hold her weight for the length of time she would need to prise off the metal cover.

The bed.

Of course. How simple. Drag the bed across to the grating and stand on that. There seemed to be no reason why she shouldn't. It only looked to be a normal single bed, and she moved one of those often enough at home when she was cleaning out her room. The only difficulty that she could see was that it might stick on the uneven floor, but she would have to chance that. She pulled at it, and it rolled easily, so easily that she had difficulty in stopping it and making it go where she wanted. By pulling at one end she managed to turn it round, so that it was pointing in the right direction and only needed a straight push to get it into position.

She started on the last few yards.

She reached the pillar that divided the two rooms.

The bed was too wide to pass between the pillar and the opposite wall.

★   ★   ★

She stopped, sitting on the edge of the bed, breathing hard with the effort of

69

pushing. There was no way in which she could get it through, but worse than that she had got it wedged, cutting herself off from the grating and stopping herself from pushing at the bed to try to free it. If the men who had kidnapped her happened to come down now, they would see what she had been doing and make sure that she couldn't use that method in future.

Almost sobbing, she tugged at the bed again, feeling it give a little, but only very slightly.

She would have to get past it somehow. If she could push it she was sure she could move it.

She climbed on to it, walking to the end where the high, slightly old-fashioned headboard was, and put one leg over it. She brought the other one up and half jumped, half fell to the ground, staggering on the stones and grazing her hand on the wall when she tried to save herself.

She cried out with the pain, the first sound that she had made since recovering consciousness.

It echoed oddly, frightening her a little.

Turning back to the bed, she pushed at it. Nothing happened until she stepped back and flung the full force of her weight against it. That shifted it, and with a low grating noise as it rubbed against the wall it moved back into the room where it had been at first.

The bloodstain was beneath it.

She shuddered when she saw it, and stepped carefully to avoid it.

Whose was it?

She hardly gave any thought to that, as she had had another idea for reaching the chute. Tearing off the bedclothes she carried them over to the heap of coal and wood that she had made earlier, and dropped them beside it. After feeling through them until she found a blanket she tugged it free of the main pile and wrapped it round and round until it made a square, compact bundle. She did the same with the one remaining blanket then laid them both on the platform and stood on them.

Her fingers just scraped the metal above her head.

She stepped down, wishing there was

another blanket, and added the sheet to the pile. It wasn't very much, even when folded into a bundle, but it might just give her the extra height that she needed.

She stood on it again.

Now she could reach the metal cover.

She pushed hard but it didn't move. For a moment she feared that it was held down by something outside, but a second bout of pushing enabled her to raise it very slightly, so slightly that she could hardly notice her achievement, except for the tiny thud that it made when she let go of it.

If only she were six inches taller!

She pushed again and again, acutely aware that the pressure was making the soft blankets settle, lowering the height of the platform with each push that she gave. If she didn't get it off soon she would have to start all over again. Fear gave her strength; suddenly she felt a cool breeze come into the cellar, and saw some stars, low down in the sky.

If only she could lift it a little more.

She pushed, standing on her toes, gasping with the effort.

Suddenly, she slipped. As she sprawled she heard the loud bang as the cover fell back into place. That sound was above her; behind her she could hear the sounds of someone coming into the cellar.

7

She was back in the bed now, back where she had started. There were two men with her, neither of them the men who had been in the car. From the way one of them talked she judged him to be American; the other was English, a clown of a man, except that his clown face didn't smile.

He said: 'It's naughty of you to try to get away, Barbara.'

So they knew her name. Somehow that made things much worse; it meant that they had kidnapped *her*, for some special reason, and not merely the first girl they had seen.

'What do you want me for?' she asked, and couldn't keep the fear out of her voice.

'You'd be surprised,' answered the American. 'You sure would.'

The clown man motioned him into silence. 'Do you know who we are?' he demanded.

Barbara shook her head.

'Are you sure?'

'Of course I'm sure.'

'Does the name Baggott mean anything to you? Ray Baggott?'

'I don't know who you are!' This time her voice rose until it was almost a scream. 'I don't know you or Ray Baggott or any of you!'

The clown man said: 'I'm Ray Baggott.'

She looked at him. He leaned closer, until she could smell the onions on his breath. She shrank away but he reached out one hand and took her shoulder.

'Don't try to get away again, Babs. It might not be nice for you when you come back.'

He let her go, pushing her back on to the bed. He had spoken softly, but there had been menace in his words, and she could make no attempt to struggle, only lie there watching him while his eyes gazed down into hers. The shoulder hurt where he had gripped it, but she felt that it would be an act of fear, of weakness, to rub it.

'What do you want me to do?' she asked finally.

'We don't want you to *do* anything,' Baggott said. 'All we want is for you to answer some questions we're going to ask you.'

She looked at the American, who was rubbing the side of his broad nose.

Baggott went on: 'And when you've done that we'll let you go. Won't we, Tex?'

Tex nodded, still rubbing his nose.

'What — what questions?'

'Not yet, Babs. You might be tempted to lie to us if we ask you now. You've got to be real anxious to answer before we can be sure you're telling the truth.' Baggott broke off, changing the subject abruptly. 'Did you know your mother was in hospital?'

'Why?' She spoke so softly that Baggott hardly heard her and had to bend close again. 'What have you done to her?'

'We ain't done nothing to her.' She smelt the onions again when he opened his mouth. 'We don't want to hurt your mother. Only you if you try to lie to us. Or if you're foolish. You were foolish

76

when you tried to get out of here. Weren't you?'

His voice rose on the last two words and he lurched forward, grabbing her arm and shaking her violently.

'Weren't you?'

'Yes,' she managed to gasp. The answer seemed to satisfy him and he released her, flinging her back on to the bed.

'You were nearly in hospital yourself,' put in the American, Tex. 'But for my friend here you could have been dead by now.'

'What do you mean?' Barbara's voice was stronger now; incredibly, some of the fear had gone. 'And what's the matter with my mother?'

'You had too much of the drug that put you out,' answered Baggott in the most reasonable sounding voice she had heard him use so far. 'I was watching your place to see what happened about the cops, and a doctor came. He sent your mother to hospital and then came here to have a look at you. He was very good.'

Barbara lay on the bed without moving. She realized that he was only telling her about her mother to upset her, to worry her and to try to stop her from thinking properly, in case she intended making up anything in answer to his questions.

What were his questions anyway?

Why didn't he ask them now and get it over with? What was it he had said? 'You've got to be real anxious to answer them.' She was anxious enough now to answer them and get out of here, to see what was the matter with her mother.

She said: 'Please ask me what you want to know and let me out of here.' The calmness in her voice surprised her.

Baggott didn't answer. He sat on the bed, looking at her, his eyes wide open in that horrible, clown like face, staring into hers. She looked back at him. He moved his face nearer, it was a mask of a face, and his eyes seemed to be growing bigger and bigger. She wanted to look away, but those eyes held her, so that she could only cower back, hoping that she was out of his reach. Slowly, almost casually, he put out his hand and took her wrist, holding it loosely between thumb and finger, changing his grip until he had the right place.

His fingers moved over the muscle, pressing, grinding.

Pain streaked up her arm.

She gasped, and tried to draw away.

He still held her, pressing harder and harder, moving his fingers all the time until the pain became unbearable.

She had to scream, the agony in her wrist and arm was so great.

Baggott let go of her. 'You've got to be real anxious to talk to me,' he repeated.

'I am anxious,' she said, trying to keep her voice steady and not show how much she was afraid of him. 'Ask me what you want to know and let me get out of here.'

'Not yet. You're still not anxious enough.'

For a moment there was silence in the room, and then it dawned on Barbara that it was the false calmness, the false assurance that she was putting into her voice that made this clown man think that she was still behaving rationally. Perhaps if she screamed and shouted at him he would ask her and let her go.

He might ask her; would he let her go afterwards?

After all, she had seen both him and the American, and knew their names. There was the bloodstain on the floor, too. It was still sticky, and that must mean that it was very new, so new that it might have been done that night. While she had been here, unconscious, someone had been murdered in this cellar.

She gasped.

The doctor who had been called to bring her round. He would have seen the men, too, and would know that they were holding her in the cellar, drugged. For their own safety they would have either had to keep him there, too, or kill him.

He wasn't here; they must have killed him.

And he had been to see her mother beforehand; in other words he must have been Mr. Franklin, the family doctor. If these men let her go now she could go to the police and tell them that they had killed Mr. Franklin.

So, once they realized that she knew, they would have to kill her, too.

The thoughts crowded into her mind until she hardly knew what she was thinking, but one thought rose above all the others. Would the men realize that she had guessed they had killed Franklin? Would they even realize that she knew that the stain was blood? In spite of her fears her eyes drifted to what she could see of it, and Baggott smiled as if this was what he had been waiting for.

'Don't think so much about that, Babs,' he advised. 'You might think things that aren't good for you to know.'

She couldn't speak, so great was the fear that he was going to tell her he actually knew what she was thinking.

Baggott said: 'She wants a drink, Tex.'

'Yeah, she wants a drink. Are we going to give her one?'

'Perhaps.' Baggott jerked his head towards the door. 'You get it.'

'Sure thing.'

Tex stood up, very tall and well built, almost handsome, Barbara thought. If she had met him in a dance hall instead of here she might have liked him, even though he was fair and she had always had something against blond men.

He left the room. She heard him climbing the steps, then came the sound of a door opening and shutting.

'Be careful, Babs,' the clown man Baggott said. 'We want answers to our questions. Good answers.'

She nodded.

'What's your name?' he rapped at her.

She feared that he was going to take her wrist again, and answered quickly: 'Barbara Young.'

Baggott grunted. 'Where do you live?'

'Risely. The new part. You know, the estate.'

Again the grunt. He seemed as if he were about to ask another question then changed his mind when he heard the American returning.

He carried a jug and a small cup, both of which he handed to Barbara. She poured water into the cup; immediately it was full Baggott took the jug from her and laid it on the floor beside the bed.

She drank from the cup, too thirsty to even think of throwing the water in Baggott's face and trying to run away.

'What do you want to know?' she asked again.

'Nothing yet, Babs. Just keep drinking.'

She finished the cup of water. Baggott took it from her and put it next to the jug.

'Right, Babs, a few things for you to think about while you're going to sleep. No one knows where you are. No one can hear you, down here. We can do whatever we want to you, and you can scream as much as you like, but no one'll hear you. Get that, Babs, and get it good if you're thinking of holding out on us.'

He shot out his hand, catching a thick bunch of hair and jerking her towards him. Pain tore at her scalp and she tried to knock the hand away but his fingers were too strong.

He was jerking her head backwards and forwards.

She screamed.

He released her and she lay still on the bed, rubbing her head.

'Anything we like,' Baggott repeated,

turning away. 'Goodnight, Babs.'

They both grinned as they went towards the door. Seconds later, the light went out.

★ ★ ★

She lay for some time in the pitch dark. With the light had gone the electric fire, and she shivered under the bedclothes.

Anything we like, Baggott had said.

Anything they liked was right, too.

She tried to sleep.

★ ★ ★

Her father was also trying to sleep. He had dozed for three hours, and at last the strain of the evening seemed about to take over, bringing sleep with it. Confused images were running through his mind. He saw Millie, her face chalk white with the two red spots and faint blue tinge on it; he saw Barbara, curled up in a chair as she would have sat had she come home; and, mixed up with all this, he saw the girl he had seen at Tim Bocking's flat, wearing the fur coat.

Almost imperceptibly, sleep came.

Outside, a car door slammed, jerking him wide awake again.

★ ★ ★

Not far away, in the rambling old house, Lil Benson lay half asleep, vaguely worried because she couldn't remember whether or not the doctor had returned. She was too warm and comfortable and sleepy to take serious notice of her fears, yet.

She turned over and was soon asleep again.

★ ★ ★

At St. Thomas' hospital, everything was quiet.

Nurse Harding had made her round of the wards, as she did every hour, and was now in the Staff Room, fluffing out her hair before the mirror on the wall. Some of the nurses regarded night duty as easy, and didn't bother to make the rounds of the wards as they should have done, but relied on the warning bells which the patients in each ward could ring if anything were wrong.

Nurse Harding liked to see for herself that nothing was wrong.

Nothing had been wrong on the last trip.

The staff room was empty except for herself. When she had finished with her hair she slipped off her shoes, which were new and hurt her feet a little, then settled down in an armchair. Her handbag was within easy reach; from it she took a thin paper-back book and began to read. Whenever she was on night duty she did this, usually managing to read two, or even three books a week this way.

She read for three quarters of an hour, then put on her shoes again and went out.

Everything was quiet until she came to Number Four Ward. The new patient was in here, the woman who had been brought in earlier that evening, just before Nurse Harding had come on duty.

Consulting her board quickly, she went to the woman's bed and flashed her torch on to the pale face. She thought that there was a flicker of movement in the seemingly lifeless face, but couldn't be sure; a second flash confirmed it. The painful shoes were forgotten now as she hurried down the ward and along the passage that led to the doctor's room. She tapped on the door, and the sound of laughter that had been coming from within ceased. A voice called out, still laughing a little, and she opened the door, peering in.

'Doctor,' she said, 'Mrs. Young is coming round if you want to see her.'

8

Harry Young awoke with an unfamiliar feeling, a sense of something missing. After he had lain for a few minutes, his eyes shut, his mind groping for an explanation, he realized what it was. The sensation of thirty-two years was missing; there was no one next to him. His wife was in hospital, ill.

He didn't even know properly what was the matter with her.

And his daughter. She, too, was missing.

Why?

Harry sat up, blinking, reached out and switched on the bedroom light, shivering slightly, for the morning was cold. He glanced at the clock. It was seven o'clock, half an hour earlier than he normally got up, but then normally he didn't have to make his own breakfast. Usually, he ate breakfast slowly, and managed to read most of the paper before he left for work.

He could still sit this morning, if he hurried, though he had no intention of leaving until he knew how Millie was.

He swung his legs out of bed, then stood up and went across to his clothes.

He felt a little less old and tired when he had dressed.

There were several things that would have to be done that day. He would have to get on the phone to Pugh, his boss, and tell him what had happened; he would have to go to the hospital and see Millie, even if she hadn't recovered, and he would have to tell Lennon's, where Barbara worked, that she wouldn't be coming in that day.

And perhaps not for many days.

Were the police taking this seriously?

Harry went downstairs, put the kettle on to boil and drew back the curtains to peer out. There was no one about, although lights were on in several of the houses opposite. A man came out of an alley between two pairs of houses; Harry knew him slightly. He was a fireman and worked odd hours. He waved when he saw Harry, then walked quickly towards the main road.

Harry let the curtain drop back into place.

The kettle wouldn't boil yet.

Taking two slices of bread from the half used loaf in the bin he put them on to toast, then hurried to remove the kettle as it began to whistle.

Everything seemed strange and unfamiliar this morning.

He had tea, buttered and ate the slices of toast, hearing the familiar thud of the paper through the letter box as he did so. Something, at least, hadn't changed. The thud seemed to jerk him back into his normal world instead of this half nightmare in which he had been living and it was with a feeling of reassurance that he picked up the paper and began to read. He half expected to see some mention of Barbara's disappearance, but there was nothing.

He couldn't tell whether he was disappointed or not.

At least if there had been something it might have shown just how seriously the police were treating this.

On impulse, he decided to include them on the list of people that he had to see that day, folded the paper and stood up, turning to go into the front room.

He saw the pale blue envelope with Barbara's name on it.

Ignoring it, he went across to his usual chair and sat down, with the feeling that he had got up too early. He wondered what time visiting started at the hospital, and what had happened to the doctor. He had promised to ring or call if there was any news about Millie, and so far there had been nothing. Of course, that might mean that there was nothing to tell, but Harry had known Maurice Franklin for many years and didn't think that he would have left things so long without some word.

He would ring the doctor before he went to the hospital.

He looked at the clock, saw that it was five to eight. Morning surgery, he knew, began at nine, so by the time he had got the car out and reached a phone box it was certain that the doctor would be up. He could ring him, go on to the hospital and speak to Pugh and Lennon's afterwards. Lennon's was on the way to the police station, so he could call there at the same time, too.

That ought to take care of everything.

He went outside and backed the car out carefully. Soon he was driving slowly towards the main road.

There was a phone box on the estate, quite near, but vandals made sure that it was constantly out of order, so rather than waste time going to see if it happened to be working he decided to use the one near the Market Hall, even though it was slightly out of his way.

Soon he arrived at the call box.

There was a woman in it. Harry stopped the car, keeping one eye on the box. The woman was gesticulating as she spoke, and a tall feather in the side of her hat bobbed up and down as she moved. Harry sat in the car; she would be a long time, he knew. Women always were in call boxes. He waited, one hand on the steering wheel, the other one in his pocket.

The woman talked.

Suddenly she put the phone down, almost slammed it down, Harry thought, and came out.

He wasn't sure, but he was almost certain that it was the woman he had seen outside Tim Bocking's flat the previous evening.

★　★　★

By the time he had decided to call her back and see if she could tell him anything, she had climbed into her car, a shiny pale blue Rover and driven off.

★　★　★

Harry went into the phone box and lifted the receiver, which was still warm from the woman's hand. A faint smell of perfume hung in the air, too. He dialled without having to look up the number; five, five, five, five. He heard the steady ringing at the other end, which seemed to go on for a long time, then a woman spoke.

'Doctor Franklin's.'

'Is the doctor there, please?'

'Who is that?'

'Harry Young.'

There was the slightest of pauses at the other end and then the woman said: 'I'm so sorry, Mr. Young, but he went out on a case last night and I haven't seen him since. Is it something urgent, or could I give him any message?'

Franklin had been out all night.

Harry's heart lurched.

His *heart*.

Millie's heart. That was what it was that had sent her to hospital. If the doctor hadn't been home all night it must mean that he had stayed at the hospital all the time, and that Millie was much worse than he had feared, so bad in fact that he didn't think it safe to leave her.

It never came into Harry's mind that the doctors at the hospital were just as competent as Franklin and that Millie would be quite safe left there, however ill she was.

He thanked the woman, hung up the phone quickly and went back to his car. If

Millie were that bad he must see her at once.

* ★ ★

He was held up badly by the thickening rush hour traffic on his way to the hospital; it took him nearly half an hour to cover a mile. At length he reached the turning, and immediately found that the traffic had vanished. He sped towards the hospital, swung in at the gates and parked his car in the forecourt.

A uniformed porter appeared.

'Will the car be all right there?' Harry asked.

'I should think so, sir. Who were you after?'

'I — my wife was brought in last night.' Even in his hurry, Harry still spoke slowly. 'I wondered where she was.'

'Know what ward, sir?'

'I'm afraid not.'

The man rubbed his chin. 'I think the reception desk will be the best place for you, sir. Follow me.'

He led him up the four wide steps at

the main entrance, and through some glass swing doors. A desk was directly opposite the doors, a young girl behind it typing slowly.

The porter went up to her.

'Gentleman here wants to find his wife, Lynn.'

The girl smiled at Harry.

'What name, sir?'

Harry told her.

She flipped through a large register next to the typewriter, then looked up.

'Number Four Ward. Does anyone know that you're coming?'

'No. She was brought in rather unexpectedly and I'd like to know how she's going on. I think that our own doctor is still with her, but I'm not sure.'

'Just a moment.' The girl turned away and pressed down a key on a telephone. She spoke into it quickly then replaced the receiver and turned back to Harry. 'Just take a seat, Mr. Young.'

Harry stepped back to the three black leather armchairs that were at the side of the desk, wondering if he had been sent out of earshot, or whether there would be just a long wait. After all, no one did know that he was coming, and there might be all sorts of things to get ready. Now that he was actually here at the hospital the need for haste and worry seemed to have lessened, and when eventually a nurse did come hurrying from a passage he rose calmly.

The nurse said: 'Mr. Young?'

'Yes. My wife — '

'She came round during the night and she's fine now. Before you see her, Sister would like a word with you. It won't take a minute.'

Harry followed the nurse along a corridor until she stopped outside a door marked 'Private', in neat black capitals on the frosted glass of the upper half. She tapped lightly on it, and a voice called to them to enter.

They went in. Sister, an elderly lady with greying hair, sat behind a large desk. A pile of X-ray photos was in front of her, some folders on the side of the desk. As they came in she brushed the pictures to one side and clasped her hands in front of her on the desk.

'Good morning, Mr. Young. I won't keep you a moment and then you can go and see your wife. She's doing very nicely.'

She had a firm, brisk voice.

As Harry sat down in the chair she indicated, she said to the nurse: 'I'll ring when I'm ready.'

'Very good, Sister.' The nurse hurried out, her starched uniform rustling.

'Now, Mr. Young, do you know of anything that has been worrying your wife?'

'Nothing until yesterday as far as I know.'

'And what happened yesterday?' The Sister spoke confidently.

'Our daughter vanished on her way home from work.'

Some of the confidence seemed to vanish. 'I'm sorry,' she said quietly. 'Has anything been heard this morning?'

'Nothing yet. I haven't been to the police so far today, so there might be something I don't know about.'

Sister tapped her nails on the blotter before her. 'This makes things more difficult, Mr. Young. The point is this. At the moment your wife is all right, but the slightest bit of extra worry will set her back, perhaps even make her worse than she was before. Do you follow me? She's going to ask about your daughter and if you tell her that she's still missing it won't help at all.'

Harry said nothing. Was this woman going to try to stop him from seeing Millie? He *had* to see her. He should have come with her last night, but he had allowed Doctor Franklin to persuade him to stay at home. Now that he was here, actually in the hospital, he was determined to see her.

He said: 'Doctor Franklin — '

Sister interrupted him. 'Have you spoken to the doctor this morning?'

Harry looked surprised. 'But surely he's here?'

'We haven't seen him. Your wife was admitted on his authority, but so far he hasn't been near the place. However, that isn't really your problem. What you're going to tell your wife is, Mr. Young.'

'What can I tell her?' Harry spread his

hands helplessly. 'If she asks I've either got to lie to her or tell her that Barbara's still missing. If she thinks Barbara's back, she'll want to see her. What do I do then?'

'Frankly, Mr. Young, I don't know what to advise.' Sister glanced out of the window, which gave on to a small grassy plot with two long seats on it. A nurse walked past the window and up some steps into a building opposite.

Harry said: 'Would it be better if I went home?'

'Don't be silly!' The woman spoke sharply. 'Now that you're here you must see her, but I don't want her worried any more than necessary. If she asks about Barbara, reassure her; tell her that the police are doing everything that can be done, that everyone is helping and so on.'

She stood up.

'Come with me.'

Harry followed her. *If* she asked about Barbara . . .

That was going to be the first thing she asked. Harry licked his lips, trying to frame a suitable reply. Were the police doing everything that they could? Were they treating it as a kidnapping or as an elopement?

That was one of the main questions.

He would find out later.

He followed Sister into the ward and along a line of beds to one at the end, with screens round it.

Screens.

Didn't they only put those round people who were seriously ill?

The antiseptic smell which Harry had first noticed when he had entered the corridor was much stronger here. At one side of the ward a woman, white coated instead of in the uniform of a nurse, was mopping the floor, with two men in brown coats sliding the beds out of position when she told them to.

They weren't near Millie.

Sister went round the screen.

Harry followed her and saw Millie, sitting up. She was wearing a nightie which he had never seen before, and for the first time it occurred to him that she would have nothing of her own here, and that it must belong to the hospital. He was suddenly confused. There was so much that he should have done before coming here; he should have brought some fruit or something, and packed a case with things she might need. Still, he could come again. This morning he had been in too much of a hurry to get here to think of anything else.

He looked at Millie.

She smiled at him; a weak smile but recognizably a smile.

'Where's Barbara?' she asked.

★ ★ ★

Lil Benson looked round at the patients in Maurice Franklin's surgery, then glanced at her watch. The doctor was very late returning from his call of the night before; usually if he were so late, he would give her a ring, but this time there had been no message. The call from Harry Young had told her that he had been there, and then on to the hospital, and, suddenly making up her mind, she went to the phone and dialled quickly.

The doctor had never been seen at the hospital.

Hesitating for only a moment after she had hung up, she took up the receiver again and dialled the local police station.

9

That was the moment when Barbara awoke. At first she couldn't remember where she was, but as soon as she opened her eyes and saw the whitewashed cellar walls, memory came flooding back. She sat up in bed, rubbing the sleep from her eyes with one hand, and yawning. Her mouth felt dry and hot, but apart from that the effects of the drug seemed to have worn off; she felt just as she always did on wakening in the morning. Her arm didn't hurt any more, either; she tried moving and flexing it.

The top of her head was sore. That was nothing to do with the drug, though; that was where the man Baggott had pulled her hair the night before, when he had said that he could do anything he liked to her and no one would know.

What did he want?

Why was he so insistent that she would try to evade his questions?

When was he going to ask the questions?

She remembered the jug of water from the night before too, and was almost certain that the men had not taken them away when they had left her. She found this to be true, and poured herself a glass thankfully, feeling much better when she had drunk it.

She was hungry.

Would the men bring her any food, or was starving her part of the treatment that would make her anxious to answer their questions?

For the first time the amount of light in the cellar puzzled her.

She knew that there were no windows, and the bulb above her head was out, but yet light came from somewhere. It didn't seem possible that so much could filter through the tiny holes in the grating; there must be a larger opening somewhere, and if there was she might be able to get out of it.

She slipped out of bed, found her shoes where they had been before and went across to the door.

It was open.

Beyond it was a flight of stairs. Licking her lips, which had gone dry again, she went up the steps, trying to hold back the thought that if she could have got out this way the men would never have left the door open. She hesitated, and it came into her mind that this might be some trick on Baggott's part to see if he could trust her to stay where she was, then she realized the foolishness of this thought. Obviously she wasn't going to stay in the cellar if she could get out; Baggott must know this, and the leaving open of the door must be an oversight.

She moved cautiously, quietly, up the stairs.

At the top, she found herself in a passage. There was no one about, and if she hurried she might be able to reach the front door, which she could see, before anyone came.

She stepped into the passage.

The door wasn't far away, about ten quick strides. There were two doors out of which people could come, but they were both shut and she might just have a chance to get there . . .

She was half-way there, actually reaching out to grasp the knob.

Baggott came out of one of the doors.

She gasped and tried to hurry forward but it was too late. Without seeming to hurry he started after her, a look of fury on his face. She grabbed at the knob, trying to turn it, but Baggott caught her shoulder and pulled her away. She struggled wildly in his grasp, but he ignored her completely, turning her and pushing her back towards the steps.

She kicked out at him.

The blow never landed. He gave her a push that sent her staggering down the last few steps, so that she thought she was going to fall, caught her roughly by her arm and spun her round to face him, still holding the arm.

'Going somewhere, Babs?' he asked pleasantly, his clown face smiling into hers without mirth.

'Of course.' Her voice was stronger than she had expected it would be. 'You don't expect me to stay down there if I can get out, do you?'

'No. On the other hand, you can't get out.'

'I can try,' she said defiantly.

He looked at her thoughtfully. 'Oh, yes, you can try, Babs, but it won't get you anywhere.'

Suddenly he pushed her backwards so that she stumbled. This time he didn't try to save her and she fell heavily, a gasp of pain forcing itself between her lips.

'Get up!'

She scrambled to her feet as the man Tex came noisily down the steps. Baggott turned to him.

'Babs wants a lesson on why she shouldn't try to get out,' he said.

With perfect teamwork the two men closed on her. She backed away swiftly but they caught her shoulders. Panting, she pushed them off, scratching with her nails. They were claws of nails, nails of which she was very proud and she saw a long red line appear down Baggott's face, heard him gasp and grunt and felt his grip loosen. She turned on the American, trying to land the points of her shoes on his shins, but he was a much bigger man than Baggott, and his long arms grasped her wrists easily, holding her where she couldn't reach him.

'Come on, Ray,' he called.

Baggott was stroking his cheek. He dropped his hand to his side and looked at her.

There was nothing clownlike about his expression now. Suddenly she was afraid, more afraid than she had ever been before in her life. Her mouth opened, her breath came in short gasps and she tried to back away.

The American held her firmly.

She felt perspiration start out on her brow.

Baggott was coming towards her very slowly, hands clenched at his sides, his lips parted slightly. Before she realized what was happening the American had stepped behind her and pulled her sharply. She was falling and cried out in fear. Someone caught her shoulders, holding them just clear of the ground, so that her legs were bent. She gave another gasp, this time of relief, and tried to struggle to her feet again. Baggott tugged at her ankles, lifting, so that she hung between the two men for a moment, then he stepped back, hoisting her legs high in the air.

She screamed.

Somehow the scream broke the tension that was in the room and in herself.

Baggott held her like that for a moment, his eyes lingering on the long, slim legs, then raised his eyes and nodded almost imperceptibly to the American.

They began to swing her backwards and forwards, so that she felt dizzy and her head swam. She wanted to scream, but something seemed to be caught in her mouth so that no sound would come.

They swung her higher and higher.

Suddenly they released her, hurling her partly on to the bed and partly against the hard stone wall. The blockage in her throat disappeared and she screamed once.

★   ★   ★

The next conscious thought that she had was of lying on the bed again. Someone

110

had straightened her out of the crumpled heap into which she had fallen before, and pulled the clothes over her, but she was aching all over, especially down her side, where she had hit the wall. She tried to twist more to the other side, so that she wouldn't be lying on the sore part, but found that she couldn't move. Filled with a sudden panic that she had been injured in some way she squirmed again, with the same lack of result.

Something was tugging at her hands every time she moved.

She realized then that she had been tied to the bed.

The old-fashioned headboard had a rail running along the top of it. A cord had been looped round each thumb and tied to this; so simple and yet so effective.

The door at the far side of the room was still open.

There was no way in which she could reach it.

She lay on the bed, tugging at the cords, but only succeeded in chafing her thumbs. After a while she stopped; if she went on like this they would be so painful that she wouldn't be able to bear being tied like this.

Where were Baggott and Tex?

When were they going to ask their questions?

But even when they asked them, it would be no help to her. If she didn't answer them they would force her to, and when they had finished they would probably kill her.

They would kill her anyway if they realized that she had guessed about the bloodstain on the floor.

She tugged again at the cords, ignoring the pain this time, and lay tossing on the bed until she heard the sound of footsteps on the stone stairs leading into the cellar. Seconds later, Baggott and Tex came in.

Baggott was smiling, as if he were amused.

They were sitting on the edge of the bed, twisted round so that they faced her.

Baggott was still smiling as he said: 'Right, Babs, I think you've learnt all your lessons. I hope you have, for your own sake.'

She looked up at him, her mouth dry.

Baggott went on: 'We know your name, we know your address. How long have you known Tim Bocking?'

Tim? Why did they want to know about Tim? What had Tim done to them, what had he to do with men like these anyway?

Baggott said: 'How long?'

'Not — not long.'

'But long enough, eh?' This was the American, also smiling mirthlessly.

'Long enough,' Baggott echoed. 'Going to get married, are you?'

'Not as far as I know. What's it to do with you, anyway?'

'You'd be surprised what a lot of things have to do with us. You haven't answered my questions yet. It won't take me long to think that you've forgotten your lessons, Babs, and that'll be too bad.'

'What do you want to know?'

'I've asked you once. How long have you known Tim Bocking?'

'And I told you,' Barbara snapped. 'Not long!'

Baggott's hand slapped across her face. She jerked her head to one side with a gasp.

'How long?'

'About two months.' The words came out hesitantly. 'I'm not sure.'

'Think, Babs.'

'I — I can't think properly with you shouting like this. You'll have to give me time.'

Baggott grinned. 'There isn't a lot of time. You ought to know better than to try a trick like that.'

'There'll have to be time,' she said boldly, aware that she might be inviting another outburst from Baggott. Whatever she did she must take as long as possible over answering these questions, must give her father and the police a chance to do something. She couldn't pretend that she didn't know the answers; obviously, she did, but she could say that she needed time to remember.

'How long, Babs? Did you know him before Christmas?'

She would have to answer this right away, it was so simple that she didn't need any time to think.

'Yes.'

'How long before Christmas was it?'

114

'About a month, I think.'

'About?'

'It might have been five weeks.' Despair sounded in her voice; she couldn't help it. 'Does it matter?'

'Leave it to us to decide what matters, Babs baby,' the American said. 'Just answer the questions and you won't get hurt. So you've known him about two months, huh?'

'I suppose so.'

'How did you meet him?' This was Baggott again.

'At a dance.'

'Where?'

'At the Community Centre.'

'Which Community Centre?'

'The — the local one. The one near Mainford Road market.'

Baggott looked at the other man enquiringly.

Tex said: 'There is one. They do have dances there from time to time.'

'Was there one about this time?'

The American stood up, heading for the door. 'I'll find out.' He left the room and she heard him climbing the steps.

Baggott remained silent while he was out of the room, gazing down at her until she felt that she could scream. She tried to look away from him, but every time she did she found that she was still aware of his intense gaze, as if he were trying to look into her mind and see the answers to his questions.

Tex came back. 'There was a dance,' he said.

Baggott nodded. 'And you met Tim Bocking at it?' he asked Barbara.

'Yes.'

'He asked you for a dance, did he?'

'Yes,' she answered hesitantly.

'You don't sound sure. Did Bocking ask you for a dance or didn't he?'

'Of course he did. You don't think I asked him, do you?'

She felt in a curious mood. Somehow it was as if now that the men had started to ask their questions a lot of her fear had evaporated. There was still a chance that they might kill her, of course, but if she could hold out for long enough the police would be sure to find her.

She remembered the dance well. She

had been dancing with someone else, and had collided with Tim and his partner, a long-haired girl with heavy make-up, three times in one dance, treading on his feet each time. At the start of the next dance he had come across and asked her, telling her that he wanted to see if she danced like that deliberately. Since then, she had been going out with him.

Baggott seemed satisfied for the moment.

Tex asked: 'And were you working for Lennon's then?'

'Of course I was, I've worked for them since I left school.'

'When was that?' Baggott asked quickly, as if he wanted to regain control of the questioning.

'Nearly three years ago.'

He grunted, looking at Tex, who was nodding his head slowly.

'And you didn't know Bocking then?'

'When?'

'Don't try to be clever, Babs.'

'I'm not. I didn't understand what you asked me.'

'Did you know Bocking when you left school?' Baggott repeated slowly.

'I've just told you that I met him at a dance two months ago. How could I have known him when I left school?' She was surprised at the strength in her voice.

Baggott stood up. Instantly all her terror came back and she wished that she hadn't spoken like that.

He reached out and gripped her hair, lifting her head from the pillow. She gasped.

Baggott said softly: 'You're forgetting your lessons, Babs. I don't want to have to teach you again.'

He let her go.

She ran her tongue over dry lips. 'What's the matter with Tim?' she asked.

'There's nothing the matter with Tim,' put in Tex. 'Oh, no, Tim's fine, just fine. It's what's the matter with Ray and Tex that worries us.'

Baggott gave him a warning look. 'Planning to get married?' he asked Barbara.

'No. I've only known him for about two months, and besides, I don't think Tim could afford to marry anyone yet.'

Tex snorted loudly, and Baggott smiled

again. 'Be careful, Babs,' he warned. 'Does Bocking want to marry you?'

'I've no idea,' she answered truthfully.

'Don't give me that. Girls always know when someone wants to marry them.'

'I tell you, I don't know!' Barbara's voice rose until she was shouting. Her head was hurting, she was hungry and all the false calmness of the past quarter of an hour seemed to vanish at once. 'What's the sense of bringing me here and asking me a lot of fool questions about Tim and me and then telling me I'm wrong when I answer them?'

'There's a lot of sense, honey,' said Tex. His eyes rested on her face and then moved over her slowly. Even though she was covered by the bedclothes there was enough suggestion in his eyes to make her blush. 'There's always sense in bringing a beautiful chick like you to a cellar like this.'

Baggott gave him a sharp look. 'Not yet,' he said curtly. 'Right, Babs, one more question.' He stood up and leaned

119

over her, one hand on each side of the bed, his face very close to hers. 'Just one more question. Where is Tim Bocking now?'

The men stood, waiting expectantly.

10

Baggott said: 'Well, Babs, where is he?'

'Unless he's at home or at work, I've no idea.'

'Don't give me that!'

'But it's true! Have you tried his home?'

'Look, Babs, I've tried his home until I'm sick of it. Where is he?'

Tex said: 'Where is his home, honey?'

She twisted to look at him. 'In the flats near where I live.'

The American nodded.

She said: 'He was going on a course for a few days from his firm, but he should have been back from that yesterday.'

'That's right, Babs. We've tried the place where he was supposed to be on the course. He isn't there either.'

Baggott said: 'Don't lie to us, Babs. If you do we'll have to teach you not to.'

'I tell you, I don't know!'

Baggott looked at the American, then

jerked his head to the side of the room. The men moved away, talking in low voices so that she couldn't hear them.

She lay on the bed, her arms stretched towards the headboard, her thumbs already sore from the continual rubbing of the cords. She gnawed her lips and tried to think of some way that she could get out, but of course there was none. There had hardly been any hope before, when she had been able to get off the bed; now that she was bound, it was more or less impossible.

Her mother came into her mind. Up to now, events had forced her to concentrate on herself, but now that she could think of other things she remembered that her mother was ill in hospital. She must get out of here, must see what was happening. What was her father doing? With both of them missing he would be in the house on his own; he had probably never had to cook his own meals before, and he would be dreadfully worried about the two of them.

She had to get out.

Baggott came over, alone.

'Listen, Babs,' he said reasonably, 'why lie to us? We could hurt you a lot, you know. You'd have to tell us in the end, why not do it now and then you can go?'

She didn't believe him for a minute. Even if he didn't realize that she had guessed about the murder he must know that the minute she got out of here she would go straight to the police and give them the address and the names of the two men. Even without the murder thrown in, it was too risky for them to let her go.

Yet from the way Baggott spoke, there was hope.

She frowned at him.

Baggott said: 'You don't think we'll let you go, do you?'

She shook her head. The minute she told them, or they guessed that she didn't know where Tim was, they would kill her.

On the other hand, how could she hold out for much longer? Her mind was dazed and confused, but not so dazed and confused that she didn't realize what these men would do to get the truth if she said nothing. Could she make them think she knew but had forgotten? Would that work to her advantage? Could she even bring it off?

She said: 'Please leave me alone. I can't think, I can't remember anything while you're like this. I'm so hungry, too. I must have time and something to eat.'

'Time is what we haven't got, Babs. You'll have to think.'

The American spoke in a surprisingly mild voice. 'She could be right, Ray. After all, we have tensed her up a lot since we got her. Give her some grub and leave her for a bit.'

Baggott turned. 'How long?' he demanded.

'Half an hour, say?'

'Half an hour? You on Bocking's side or something?'

On Bocking's side, she thought. What sides were there? And why should Tim be on any side at all?

Had he vanished, as they had said?

She said: 'I can't think about anything,' and moaned as if she were in pain.

The American said: 'Better leave her, Ray. Course, if she doesn't tell us after we'll have to really get to work on her.

But give her chance first.'

'Give her chance,' Baggott repeated softly. 'Give her chance! Don't you think I've given enough people chances? Don't you think I gave Bocking enough chance? And look what he's done to us. You fool, can't you see that she's in league with Bocking? That's what she's trying to do, she's trying to give him time to get away.'

Barbara lay on the bed, trying not to draw Baggott's rage on to herself. She knew that he must be raving now, as if she had wanted Tim to get away, he had had all night and most of the previous evening. In fact, since he must have been missing for some time when she had been kidnapped he had had since six o'clock the previous evening to disappear.

What need was there to give him more time?

Another thought occurred to her. Tim must have been missing for a lot longer than that if he hadn't been on the course. Why should they think that she knew where he was? Why were they certain enough of it to have her drugged and kidnapped?

The American said: 'He's already had enough time to get away, Ray. Another half hour won't make all that much difference. He must have told honey girl here where he was going. She'll tell us in the end.'

He stopped, as the knocking at the front door began to throb throughout the cellar.

* * *

For a moment no one moved.

Baggott was the first to recover. 'It must be Clare,' he said, though his voice lacked conviction.

'Why should she come here? There's no reason. She'd have told us she was coming when she rang, if it was her. It must be someone else.'

Baggott nodded slowly.

Tex said: 'What do we do with the girl?'

'Never mind the girl yet. What are we going to do about that?' Baggott jerked his thumb towards the steps and the door at the top.

'You'll have to answer it. You'll have to

hide the girl while you do it.'

'Can't we leave it?'

The American shook his head. 'I guess it's safer to answer it. Someone might know we're here.' He turned to Barbara. 'You'll have to make sure she can't shout.'

Baggott stepped very close to the bed. Barbara twisted away, but the cords round her thumbs restricted her movement.

'If you come any nearer I'll scream.'

'Scream,' Baggott invited. 'No one can hear you till the doors open.' Almost leisurely he took a handkerchief from his pocket. 'We'll have to gag you.'

The knocking came again, loud and insistent.

Official sounding knocking.

Barbara screamed: 'No!'

Baggott grabbed a handful of her hair, lifting her head with it. She opened her mouth to shout again and he rammed the handkerchief into it. She moaned while he tucked it in carefully, making sure that there were no loose ends hanging out. She tried to swallow, and choked, sure that the cloth was going to slip into her throat and stop her from breathing. Tex was passing another cloth across; Baggott tied this one round her face, so that the first one was held firmly and there was no chance of her pushing it out.

He released her.

Her head fell back on to the pillows. She lay looking up at them, and tried to scream. Her throat hurt, but the sound that came out was so low pitched that it couldn't have been heard more than a yard away.

Baggott was going up the stairs.

Any minute now he would open the front door. Help would be only a few feet away and she was helpless to shout for it. She moaned into the gag again while Tex looked at her.

'Quiet, honey,' he said. 'You'll have to be taught a lesson if you're not careful.'

She turned her head towards him, feeling the cloth tight round her face when she moved, then looked away.

She heard voices at the front door.

Baggott's voice, and then the caller.

'Good morning,' the newcomer said. 'I'm sorry to trouble you but I wonder if you saw this car anywhere around here last night.'

A pause, while the man was obviously showing Baggott the picture, then: 'I don't think so, officer. What's the reason?'

'Investigating a murder, sir. The car belonged to a doctor who's vanished.'

'He was murdered, was he?' Baggott asked, his voice elaborately casual, it seemed to Barbara.

The caller, evidently a policeman, coughed. 'Should have said suspected murder, really, sir. There's no evidence of death yet, but the man's vanished and his car was last seen round here sometime last night. There was no reason why he should want to disappear and we're assuming for the moment that he's been killed.'

'I see,' Baggott said. 'Had any luck yet?'

Baggott's question came clearly to the two people in the cellar. Tex looked at the girl tossing on the bed, her eyes wide with the effort of trying to free herself from the cords; she took no notice of him.

The policeman said: 'Not yet, sir. Plenty of time yet.'

'I suppose there is.' Baggott's voice sounded hoarse and breathy now. 'Well, the best of luck. Too many murders these days. Hope you get him.'

There came the sound of the door slamming.

Seconds later Baggott's footsteps clattered on the steps.

He came into the cellar and almost ran up to Tex. Now that help had gone Barbara lay still again, listening to what Baggott was saying.

'The cops. They're on to this place, I'm sure.'

'That was the doc's car I suppose?'

Baggott nodded. 'What did you do with it?'

'Don't fret yourself, no one'll find it or him. What makes you think they're on to here?'

'You heard what he said. A case of murder. How do they know it's murder and that the doc hasn't just ran out? Answer me that! How do they know it's murder?'

'Quit worrying,' Tex said. 'You asked him that and he told you, remember? He said that they didn't know but that they were assuming it was because the man had no reason to disappear. Quite right, too, if he'd been to the Young's. If he was going to vanish he wouldn't do it while he was out on a call. We didn't think of that, that's all.'

'What else haven't we thought of?' Baggott demanded harshly. 'Tell me that?'

'You really want to know, Ray?' The American's voice was mild.

Baggott's hands clenched. His breath rasped. 'Well?'

'We've forgotten about the chick. Babs honey has heard everything you, me and the cop have said. If she's any sense at all she'll know exactly what happened here last night.'

Baggott swallowed. 'We'll have to kill her now,' he said, turning to look at Barbara.

*　*　*

The American grabbed Baggott's arm.

'Not yet,' he insisted. 'Later.'

Barbara looked at the bigger man, fear

131

and puzzlement mingling in her eyes. Somehow it seemed as if Tex were always protecting her, almost as if he wanted to be friendly with her. She must watch this and see if she could use it in some way, later, to escape, but for the moment there was hope in the police. If they had got so far, so soon, there was plenty of hope. If only she could stall the men a little longer, until the police came back. She was sure that they would be back; if they had brought Doctor Franklin's car here last night, someone in the street would have seen it outside the house and would be sure to tell the constable. Once he knew that, he would come back, with others, and they would insist on making a search of the house.

Baggott said: 'We'll have to get her away from here.'

'I can see that. Where can we take her?'

'What about Clare?'

Tex shrugged his shoulders. 'I wouldn't. I don't know why, but I wouldn't. Madge, yes.'

'She wouldn't like it.'

'I couldn't care less whether she likes it

or not,' Tex replied. 'Look, Ray, how long was the Jew boy's car outside last night?'

'About half an hour,' Baggott answered.

'Right. In that time someone's sure to have seen it. They've only got to tell that flick and we'll have the whole pack of them back here with a search warrant before the morning's out. In fact, it wouldn't surprise me really if that *was* a try on, like you said. We're going to have to be very careful about this.'

He considered, then said:

'You're right, Madge won't like it. So, we have to sweeten her a bit.'

'How?' Baggott demanded.

'I don't know. We can't kill her, too. There are too many people being killed for me, already.'

Barbara looked from one to the other, her disappointment making tears prick at her eyes. If they moved her there would be no chance of being found. By good luck the police had got on to this place; it was unthinkable that they should have the same luck twice. Once she was moved she would be on her own again.

There was something else, too.

The name Madge was completely unfamiliar to her, but she had heard of someone called Clare before.

She couldn't remember where.

The gag was choking her.

She tried to swallow, tried to push the obstruction away with her tongue, and managed to get a little relief. If they left her for any length of time she was sure she would suffocate.

Baggott was saying: 'Suppose we offer Madge a bigger cut?'

Who was Madge? Would she help, if Baggott didn't sweeten her enough? And who was Clare? Barbara had a feeling that Clare could be important, that she was someone who could explain quite a lot.

'How much?' Tex asked quickly.

'Not as much as you think. Of course, we needn't ever pay it to her. Once we know where Bocking is Madge needn't see either of us again.'

Barbara twisted to look at him.

He grinned at her. 'Don't think you can hold out for long, kid.'

She turned away and the American

said: 'We'll have to hurry.'

'That's right,' repeated Baggott. 'We'll have to do something about Madge. And there isn't much time!'

His voice rose shrilly.

11

Tex said: 'Don't panic, Ray. That was always your trouble, wasn't it?'

'So what are we going to do?'

'We're going to get out of here and go to Madge's. There, we can work on honey child until she tells us what we want to know.' He turned and grinned at Barbara.

'And what if Madge objects?'

'Madge won't have anything to say about it. Have you ever known her to object?'

Without waiting for an answer the American crossed the cellar to the door and ran lightly up the steps. Barbara heard him open the door at the top and then the sound of footsteps hurrying down the passage. There was a short pause before he returned.

'We'll have to be careful,' he said to Baggott. 'The cops are watching the house.'

'Watching the house!'

'Yeah.'

'How many of them?'

'Shut up and let me think.' The American sat down on the edge of the bed, his weight making the springs bounce up and down. Barbara moved slightly, to try to ease the growing pain in her thumbs, caused by the cords.

No one took any notice of her.

Tex spoke slowly. 'The cops can't be watching the house. If they are then that means that they suspect something but they haven't enough proof to do anything. That's fine, as long as we don't give them any proof.'

'How have they got here?' Baggott demanded.

'They saw the doc's car, or somebody did,' Tex answered. 'Don't panic, it isn't serious.'

Barbara thought: if the police are watching, then they can't take me outside without being seen. If they are seen, then they'll want to know what the men are doing and I can escape that way. If they don't take me outside, then the police will be back again soon anyway.

Either way, there would soon be an end to this nightmare.

Tex said: 'There isn't much time.'

Baggott was standing by the pillar that separated the two rooms. At the other man's words he turned and came across to the bed, gripping Tex by the shoulders. 'How many cops are there?' he demanded.

'Two as far as I can see, one at each end of the block.'

'In cars?'

'Nope. That makes things easier. What we gotta do is distract them while we get the kid out. Once we're away from here they can do what they want.' He paused as a sudden idea struck him. 'There's nothing here that can put them on to Madge, is there?'

'Baggott shook his head. 'Nothing to put them on to her or on to us. You know that.'

The American nodded. 'If only there were three of us,' he muttered slowly.

'Why three?'

'So that two of us could draw the cops away while the third takes the kid as soon

138

as the coast is clear.' He began to walk slowly towards the steps.

From where she lay Barbara could just see him. His hands were behind his back, his head bowed and his lips set in a firm line. She had often seen her father like that, when there had been some difficult household decision, or when he had been thinking about something from work.

That was the only similarity between this man and him.

Why did they want Tim?

She tossed the question around in her mind, trying to think of anything he had done in the short time that she had known him that might give a clue as to what the men were after, but there was nothing. Trying to keep her mind clear and to concentrate on this helped the feeling of terror to go away, she found, and she began to go through everything they had done, with deliberate thoroughness.

The first time she had seen him had been at the dance. He had been dancing most of the evening, not with the same girl, but with two or three, until she had collided with him all those times in the same dance. After that, he had come to her, and made an excuse to stay with her when the music ended. She had not objected to this; how could she with someone like Tim? He had kept her amused throughout the dance, he was passably good looking, and he danced marvellously.

She wouldn't have admitted it to anyone, but the fact that he stayed with her, though obviously having a lot of partners to choose from, went a long way towards keeping her at his side.

Only one thing had spoiled that first evening, and that had been an argument that Tim had had with another girl there. Barbara had kept to one side while it was going on, and Tim hadn't mentioned it again until nearly a week after, when he took her out.

She drew her breath in with a gasp, causing Baggott to turn and stare at her.

Tim's words ran through her mind.

He had said: 'Don't worry about what Clare said at the dance. She's often like that for no reason.'

140

Clare!

She wondered why she had never realized it before, and put it down to the blockage in her mind caused by her fear. Tim had known this girl called Clare, and she worked for Lennon's. In fact, she was her boss's secretary, Clare Roberts.

But how could Clare Roberts be involved with these men?

She tried to recall everything she knew about her, but that wasn't much. Their work didn't bring them much into contact, and Clare was frequently out of the office, on some errand for the boss. On the occasions when she had tried to raise the subject with Tim, she saw now how cleverly he had turned the conversation on to something else.

So the key to this mystery must lie with Clare. Or must it?

On the nights when he hadn't seen her, she had assumed that Tim was where he said he had been, at night school studying for an accountancy qualification, but in the light of these new facts that wasn't necessarily true. He could have been anywhere; with Clare, or even with

141

Baggott and Tex. As this realization filled her mind, she pulled involuntarily at the cords which bound her, and pain streaked through her thumbs. She gave a little moan into the gag, and Baggott looked at her, hate in his eyes.

She swallowed, pushing at the cloth with her teeth as it threatened to slip into her throat and choke her.

Baggott came across, standing as he had done before, one hand on each side of the bed.

'Don't try to be clever, Babs,' he warned her.

She turned her head so that she didn't have to look at his eyes; after standing there motionless for a moment he turned and walked away.

Tim came back into her mind.

She wasn't in love with him, or anything like that. At nineteen, she had thought of getting married, of course, but not yet; in any case, as she had already told the men, she didn't think that Tim could have afforded to marry anyone. Was that why they had laughed? Had he been involved in something with them, and had he really much more money than she thought?

He always managed to find the money to take her out, sometimes to quite expensive places, although from what he had told her about his job he wasn't very highly paid. Never had she known him have to work out how much money he had got left, as some of her boyfriends had had to do often; he ran a motor scooter and he lived on his own in a flat.

Could he do all that on the low salary he was supposed to get?

Was there really any ground for suspecting him like this, or was it just the effect that Baggott and the American were having on her?

Her thoughts were interrupted by Tex, who snapped his fingers and said: 'Got it!'

★ ★ ★

Instantly Baggott looked across at him.
'Well?'

The American said: 'Go and ring Madge and ask her to take the car to somewhere near here, say the call box at the Market Centre. She can ring us when she's there; I'll leave here then, walk to the car, and one cop will follow me. When I get there, I'll ring you. You leave, I'll come back in the car and take the girl. If we work fast enough, both the cops will be away from the house for long enough.'

'Two things that I can see,' Baggott said. 'What if the cops aren't watching us? In that case it won't make any difference how many times we go out, they won't follow us. They'll just stay here, watching the street. And what if they do follow us? Others'll come to take their places.'

'I thought of that. If they aren't watching us then we're all right, because they won't take any notice of us. As for the other thing, we'll just have to work pretty fast, before any other cops have chance to get here.'

Baggott shrugged. 'It's your plan.'

'That's right, it's my plan. That's why it'll work. Now go and ring Madge.'

Baggott left the room, hurrying up the steps as if he had suddenly remembered that there wasn't much time.

When he had gone, Tex crossed to

Barbara, and sat on the edge of the bed. 'Why don't you tell us, kid?' he asked softly. 'You'll make things a lot easier for yourself if you do.'

She looked up at him, the gag tight around her mouth.

'Nod your head if you want to tell me now.'

She didn't move.

The American's expression hardened. 'You sure, kid?'

Still she didn't move. How could she offer to tell him where Tim was when she didn't know? He had been away for a few days, supposedly on this course, but he should have been back now. He had rung her at Lennon's yesterday, before she had been kidnapped; she had assumed then that he had been ringing from his flat, but of course he could have been anywhere.

'Okay.' Tex stood up. 'I shall sure hate spoiling that pretty face and figure of yours.'

He went into the other room, the one where the grating was that she had tried to lift. He had done this on purpose, she knew, so that she would have nothing to think about other than what he had just said. She lay back on the bed, feeling tears pricking at her eyes again. Somehow the fact that she didn't even love Tim made this worse; that she should have to suffer all this for a man about whom she felt very little really. How could she tell them, how could she persuade them that she was telling the truth?

There were two hopes yet. One was Madge, who might be persuaded to stop them, and the other was the fact that to move her they would have to untie her, and she might be able to make some kind of an attempt then.

The American came back.

He carried a knife.

A fresh wave of fear came over her, that he wasn't going to wait until they got to Madge's but was going to start now. Perhaps that was why he had sent Baggott away; so that whatever he learnt he would be able to keep to himself.

He stood over her, the knife blade slanting downwards, the light catching it, hurting her eyes when it flashed.

She expected to see it slash her face at any moment.

To her surprise he lowered it very slowly and cut the cords that bound her thumbs.

She would have to try now, she knew. As soon as the cords fell loosely she swung her feet off the bed and began to run. The American was too surprised to stop her, and she hadn't been on the bed for long enough to lose the use of her legs; before he realized what had happened she was almost at the door.

'You minx!' he roared, and she heard him coming after her.

Too late she realized that she had left her shoes behind, and with them a valuable weapon. She was defenceless against his greater strength now; there was only speed to rely on. If he threw his knife he would be certain to catch her, but on the other hand he wouldn't want to take any chance of killing her.

She stumbled up the steps.

Unless he were an expert with the knife he wouldn't use it; if he was an expert there was no chance of getting away. As she ran she expected to feel the sharp pain of it slicing into her legs, and she gasped into the gag in an attempt to draw in enough air to breathe. Her legs were weaker than she had realized, too, and there was just a twinge of cramp in them.

The gag was preventing her from breathing. She would have to stop soon, to rest her legs, and to breathe.

She tore at the knot, but it held firmly.

At the top of the steps she hesitated fractionally. She had no idea what she was going to do, her one idea was to get away, and the best plan seemed to be to head for the front door. Opposite to her was the door she had seen before, when she had tried to sneak out that morning. It seemed much further away now than it had then, and the American's footsteps sounded very loud behind her.

She had to reach it.

She was choking with the gag.

Baggott came out of the door, just as he had done that morning. He gaped, and then reacted much faster than Tex had done in the cellar, stepping so that he was right across the passage.

She turned, just as swiftly, and went through the other door that opened off the passage. As long as she was free she would make a chance to get to the front door, or to a window.

The room she was in was much smaller than she had expected and was furnished only with a chest of drawers and an easy chair. Banging the door behind her, she ran to the chair, tugging at it. It was heavier than it looked and although it would be ideal if she could drag it across the door it would be nearly impossible to move it in the short time that she had.

Stairs opened off one side of the room.

As the door burst open behind her and the men dashed in, she raced for the stairs. Breath whistled through her nose, her dress felt very tight, so tight that she could hardly run. She must reach the stairs. Once there, the men could only come up one at a time, and she would have a chance of throwing things at them, or of pushing them back down again.

She reached the bottom stair, felt someone very closely behind her, and almost threw herself forward.

She stumbled. Behind her she heard a cry, then something heavy struck her across the back of the legs. It was a hand. She knocked it away as the fingers bent and clutched, fear giving her strength, and stumbled on.

There were no sounds behind her now.

When she reached the top she cast a terrified glance over her shoulder, and saw Baggott sprawling across the narrow stairs, with Tex bending over him. Quickly she went into one of the bedrooms. Here, there was a bed, blankets piled on it in a heap, a large wooden armchair in one corner, and another scratched chest of drawers.

She dragged the chair across to the door. This time she might get away; there would be time to pull everything across the door as the men were still at the bottom of the stairs. If she could do that, then open one of the windows, she would be able to shout or scream, and someone would be certain to hear her. After that, she would have nothing to fear.

The chest of drawers was disappointingly light, as if all the drawers were empty, and made a hollow rumbling sound as it was pulled across the floor and wedged next to the chair. The bed was the only thing left now; by the time she had finished moving that she was hot and sticky with perspiration, but at least there was a solid barricade at the door.

She wanted a rest, but there was no time.

She turned to the window, anxious to open it and shout to the policemen before Tex and Baggott smashed their way in. Now that there was a little time, she reached behind her and tugged at the knot of the gag.

From the door came the first thud as the men began to smash it down.

12

She couldn't undo the gag.

The knot at the back of her head, which pressed tightly against the flesh, was too firm for her to manage unaided. She pulled at it desperately, then tried to work the cloth out of her mouth. More thuds sounded at the door; looking round she actually saw the bed move a few inches.

She gave a little sob and tugged again.

Suddenly she realized that the main cause of the trouble was that she was trying to do things too quickly. Calm down, she told herself. Forcing herself not to hurry was a strain, but she managed to lower her hands and keep them at her side until the trembling, which had started some time ago, ceased. Her breathing was easier now, too; she no longer had the choking feeling. At length she reached up again to the knot. There wasn't much time left. The bed had moved at least a foot, and she could see the chest of drawers rock slightly under the blows.

Soon, the men would be in.

Almost calmly she pushed at the knot, until she managed to hook one fingernail under the cloth. She pulled, gently at first but with increasing force, until, gradually, she felt it working free. She was sure that there wouldn't be time to get it off, open the window and attract the attention of one of the policemen before the barricade at the door gave way.

The knot came free.

She threw the cloth on the floor and worked the handkerchief out of her mouth.

The chest of drawers tottered and began to fall.

As it crashed to the floor she realized that there was only the chair keeping the men out, and ran back to the door. Frantically she pushed the bed, but the door was half open, and Baggott's foot prevented it from closing. Had she had her shoes on, she could have dug the pointed toes and heels into him, but barefoot she was helpless.

She thudded the bed against the door as hard as she could, almost sobbing with fear as Baggott forced the opening a fraction wider. The chest of drawers slid forward sluggishly, and she heard a faint tinkling sound. Looking down, she saw a knife, identical to the one the American had, and thought at first that he had thrown his into the room. As this was unlikely, she guessed that it had been in one of the drawers and had fallen out. She stooped and snatched at it. Baggott's hand was round the edge of the door now, forcing it open slowly. Hardly realizing what she was doing, she hacked at the fingers. There was a scream, the hand vanished, and she managed to shut the door.

Blood showed, smeared faintly on the edge.

As she rammed the chest of drawers and the bed back into place she heard the American's voice clearly, in spite of the door between them.

'Come on out, honey, it'll be easier in the long run.'

She didn't answer, but ran to the window, still holding the knife. It was an old-fashioned type of window, which lifted instead of opening out, and for a horrible moment she wondered if it would be stuck, as that type of window often was. As soon as she tried it all her fears went; the window opened easily.

She brushed the curtains aside and looked out into the street. The fresh breeze blew on to her face, heavenly after being locked in the cellar for so long, and the sun shone weakly.

There was no policeman anywhere in sight.

There was no one at all in the street.

At first she didn't realize what this meant, thinking that she would only have to scream to attract attention to herself; suddenly the realization dawned that there was no one whose attention she could attract.

She screamed.

There was no sign that anyone had heard her.

She heard the American's voice again. 'If those cops hear her . . . '

More thuds at the door. Another scream.

Still no one seemed to have heard her. She didn't recognize the street in any way, so there was no chance of telling where she was. All the houses were old, with tall bay windows and attics, most of them badly in need of a coat of paint. The only thing which moved was a dog at one end of the road, snuffling round a sheet of newspaper. Not far away she could see what looked like a shop, but there was no one in sight.

She heard the chest of drawers fall again and turned to see what was happening.

The bed was being thrust back into the room under the pressure on the door. She realized that she would either have to let them catch her again, or she would have to climb out of the window.

★ ★ ★

Where could she go if she did climb out?

★ ★ ★

She ran across and peered out. The bedroom was at the front of the house, and apart from the narrow sill there was the top of the bay, if she could reach it. However, even to her panic-stricken eyes it didn't look safe; she could imagine herself plunging through if she tried to jump down on to it. One of the boards was missing completely, while two of the others were rotten and broken.

While she hesitated she heard the sound of one of the men coming into the room.

She turned to face him. It was the American, racing across the floor. She thrust her head out of the open window, opening her mouth to scream, but before she had uttered a sound a hand pressed hard against her teeth and she was lifted bodily and swung across the floor.

Her last view from the window was of a man coming out of the shop.

The American flung her on to the bed, face down, forcing her head into the pile of blankets so that she felt she was suffocating. She struggled wildly to free herself. All sounds now were muffled, but she thought she could hear someone else coming into the room. This would be Baggott, whose fingers she had hacked with the knife. She still felt a sense of savage pleasure at having done that, but mingled in with it was the greater sense of terror.

What would he do to her now?

She couldn't breathe. The American was pressing harder, so that the pressure itself was painful, while her chest ached from trying to draw in air. She kicked out and beat at the mattress with one of her hands; the other one was trapped beneath her body.

She heard a thud as Baggott closed the window, and knew that it wouldn't be long before he came over to her.

A wave of dizziness swept over her.

Dimly, she could feel something rough at her ankles, then something pulled and drew tight; they were binding her legs. For a moment the awful pressure on the back of her head relaxed, but only for a moment, while they pulled out the hand that was beneath her.

They bound her wrists.

Only then did the American pull her head out of the smothering bedclothes. She gasped in great breaths of air, her mouth open wide. Before she had time to realize what they were doing, Baggott had pushed the cloth back into her mouth and tied the gag again.

She could only lie, looking up at them. She knew from the look on Baggott's face that, but for the American, he would kill her.

★   ★   ★

The American said: 'Not yet, Ray.'

Not yet . . .

Baggott said what she knew he would say. 'She wants another lesson, Tex.'

'All right, Ray, you give her her lesson, but remember that we want to talk to her when you're through.' He crossed to the window. 'Did anyone take any notice of her?' He peered out, then came back to the centre of the room, apparently satisfied. 'What's Madge doing?'

'She's going to ring us when she gets there.'

'Well she ain't rung yet. When she does, I'll get off and you can deal with honey child. I can't see any of the cops about now; you might be able to shift her while I'm gone.'

Baggott said: 'Seems a waste of time for you to go in that case.'

'Perhaps it is.' Tex shrugged. 'Listen, Ray, if you wanna teach her a lesson while I'm out, remember that she's gotta talk after it.'

Somewhere in the house a phone bell began to shrill.

★ ★ ★

Baggott left the room, hurrying slightly, looking as if he were afraid that the sound would cease before he got there. After another look at Barbara, the American followed him.

As soon as they had gone she began to struggle, trying to free herself from the bonds. The moment that Tex left the house, she would be alone with Baggott for at least quarter of an hour. What would happen to her in that time she

160

didn't know, but there was no indications that she would be spared anything.

She had to get out.

Gradually she realized that she couldn't.

★   ★   ★

While Barbara tossed on the bed upstairs Baggott was speaking into the phone in the front room downstairs. Finally he hung up and turned to Tex.

'Any time now, Tex.'

'She's there?'

'That's what I said, isn't it?' Baggott spoke harshly, nursing his injured hand from which the blood still ran.

'That's what you said,' Tex agreed, 'but you're likely to say anything, the mood you're in.'

'I just want to teach that minx not to stab me.'

The American laughed. 'Sure you do. I want a go at her myself.' His voice was light. Without warning he reached out, grabbing hold of Baggott's collar, almost lifting him off his feet. 'Look, Ray, leave the kid alone while I'm out, okay?'

'Why?'

'Because it's all very well to talk about teaching her a lesson but you might just decide to do a bit of a double cross while you're at it. Mightn't you, huh?'

'What do you mean?' Baggott made no attempt to free himself.

'You know what I mean, bub. It might just be that while you're teaching her a lesson she decides that the only way to stop you is to tell what she knows. That'd be real smart for you, wouldn't it, Ray? Croak the kid and get after Bocking, leaving me to stew! Well it ain't going to happen that way. You try and double cross me and I'll kill you, Ray!' His voice rose. 'Do you hear, I'll kill you!'

He flung Baggott from him and left the room.

★   ★   ★

Upstairs, Barbara's terror mounted as the footsteps on the stairs came nearer. To her they seemed to move with a kind of measured deliberateness, as if the person who was coming were desperately angry

162

but was determined to waste none of it by stamping up the stairs.

She had ceased the futile struggle to escape.

The door opened; she had expected Baggott, and was surprised to see the American.

He crossed to the bed with the same measured tread. 'Listen, honey, if Baggott lays a finger on you while I'm out, you tell me, huh?'

She nodded, eyes wide open; staring at him.

He gave a curt nod and went back down the stairs, hurrying now. Minutes later the door slammed. No one else came up the stairs for a long time.

★ ★ ★

The next sound she heard was the ringing of the phone bell, followed by a long silence.

She didn't know that she was alone in the house.

★ ★ ★

Baggott hurried, followed by the policeman in plain clothes. When he reached the Market Hall, Baggott paused, looking round for Tex. When he saw him, he crossed to him. The American ignored him, and hurried through the double swing doors that led into the large, crowded Hall itself. Stalls were ranged on all sides, exactly as in a market. Most of them were selling cheap goods that people would buy on the spur of the moment, but one of them had carpets, another was piled with expensive cut glass ware. Tex went to one of the more popular stalls, which was crowded with people, and worked his way into the crowd. Baggott followed him, and took the car keys from the hand that surreptitiously held them out. When he had them he went back to the entrance, saw one of the plain clothes men hovering around, and stepped outside.

The police were on to them all right; the man followed.

Baggott went to a blue car parked in the road, the number plates covered with dirt and mud. He climbed in, started the engine and drove off.

Behind him, the plain clothes man stared then hurried to a phone box.

* * *

Barbara knew that the footsteps on the stairs could only belong to Baggott, and involuntarily she tensed. In spite of what the American had said, she didn't think that she would be safe from the clown-like Baggott, and she tensed even more when he came into the room and strode over to the bed. Without a word, he leaned over her, picking her up. She moaned into the gag as he almost dropped her, then she sensed that he was holding her firmly.

He carried her down the stairs and she still had enough reason left to see the sense of not struggling with him here.

In spite of the fact that he frequently changed the positions of his hands as he walked she felt that he was holding her easily and without strain. Her head lolled and once struck the banister painfully, but she managed to remain silent, not wanting him to see that he had hurt her. Once, she felt his hand on the bare skin of her thigh; she even managed to bear this without whimpering into the cloth.

At length they were in the hallway. He laid her on the carpet, opened the front door and peered out. When he was satisfied that no one was around, he picked her up again and carried her out to a waiting car, the door already open.

Soon she was laid on the back seat. The whole thing had been done so neatly and quickly that she doubted if anyone could have noticed anything.

Baggott drove swiftly. Barbara, on the back seat, was flung around on the corners, and it was one of his faster corners that gave her the glimmer of a chance of getting away. The car rolled particularly heavily, and her feet were flung over the edge of the seat cushion. She thought that she was going to fall, but managed to choke back the whimper just in time, and lie half on and half off the seat.

Moving cautiously, so as not to attract Baggott's attention, she worked her feet until they were flat on the floor and there was no longer any danger of falling, then sat up slowly.

Soon they would have to stop at traffic lights or somewhere and then someone would be certain to see her.

She turned her face to the window, and moved closer to the glass.

She saw her father.

Something hard struck her in the back of the neck. Before she had had chance to attract her father's attention, Barbara fell back on to the seat, unconscious.

13

Harry Young walked quickly, having spent longer at the hospital than he had expected, and now finding that he would have to rush to finish all his jobs that morning. Lennon's, where Barbara worked, was his next call. He had been to the police, and had been pleasantly surprised to find the case was being treated as an urgent one, connected with the disappearance of Maurice Franklin. They wouldn't tell him any more than that, but that was enough to reassure him.

Millie, too, had been easy to satisfy. When she had asked her inevitable question about Barbara, Harry had spoken in his slow and deliberate way.

'I've told the police, love. They're doing all they can and I'm sure that they'll soon have her back, safe.'

There was no sense in telling her that Barbara had come back if she hadn't, however much it might help her to recover. What would happen if she found out that there was no truth in it? What would happen if — the question came into his mind almost as quickly as the other, although he tried to push it away.

What would happen if she never came back?

He glanced over his shoulder to see if the road was clear before crossing. The shiny blue car that he saw was just another car to him; he waited for it to pass, then carried on walking.

★   ★   ★

In his office at Lennon's, John Little dictated a letter to a typist. She sat opposite to him on a hard wooden chair, the only one in Little's tiny office other than the padded one he sat on, and looked up from time to time when he paused to think. He finished off a letter and sat back, rubbing his small moustache with one hand.

The typist put her pad on the desk, knowing from past experience that the pause would be a long one.

The office was shady, even though the sun was shining strongly outside. At this time of the day it shone in at a window directly behind Little, making it difficult for the typist to see her book, and the cream-coloured linen blind was drawn.

A knock at the door interrupted his thoughts.

'Come in,' he called.

A young man opened the door, looking round the edge of it at Little. 'There's a Mr. Young to see you, sir. It's Barbara Young's father.'

'Mr. Young?' Little pushed his lower lip out, musing. Apart from the fact that Barbara hadn't turned up for work that morning, he knew nothing. 'All right,' he said, 'show him in.'

'Yes, sir.' The young man went out.

'That'll have to do for now.' Little smiled at the typist. 'Can you come back after lunch?'

'Yes.' The girl smiled, white teeth vivid against bright red lips. She stood up, pushed the chair to one side of the room and crossed to the blind.

170

After she had raised it she stood for a moment, looking at the block of offices opposite with eyes narrowed against the glare of the sun, then turned and went to the door.

She met Harry Young as he was shown in.

* * *

Harry recognized the girl he had seen at Bocking's flat, and later at the phone box.

She smiled as she passed.

* * *

'Good morning, Mr. Young.' Little stood up, extending his hand. 'Exceptional weather for the time of year, isn't it?'

'It is,' Harry agreed absently.

'My name's Little. What can I do for you?'

Harry sat down in the chair that Little indicated, and smiled.

'No objection to my smoking, is there, Mr. Little?'

'That depends on what you're going to

smoke.' Little paused and then smiled. 'Smoke what you like, it's all the same really, but don't tell any one I told you that.'

Harry took out his pipe, tamped down the tobacco and lit up. Lennon's was one of the biggest tobacco wholesalers in London, and for a moment the serious-ness in Little's voice had been startling. When the pipe was going satisfactorily, Harry said:

'I've come about my daughter.'

Little frowned. 'Ah, yes. No trouble, I hope? Shouldn't like to lose her, you know, she's very good.'

'No, no trouble,' Harry replied. 'At least, not in the way you probably mean.' He leaned forward, nearer the desk. 'The fact is, Mr. Little, she's vanished.'

'Vanished?'

'Hasn't come home. The last we saw of her was yesterday morning, before she left for work.'

For a moment there was silence in the office. Harry pulled on his pipe, looking out of the window, his eyes screwed up against the glare of the sun, unexpected and pleasant at this time of the year. He could see the windows of the office block opposite; one of them had fresh, white lace curtains at it, while the remaining two had large 'To Let' notices, printed a glaring red on white, stuck in them.

Little said: 'She left here at her usual time last night. I recall that she was very excited because her exam results were waiting for her. In fact, I promised her another pound a week if she'd passed.'

'Yes, she told us.'

Little tapped on the desk, looking a shade embarrassed. 'I'm not quite sure how to put this, Mr. Young. Don't take me the wrong way.' He laughed, shortly. 'I'm not married myself, so I've no daughters and I don't know much about them, but, well, there's no chance that she's gone off with that boyfriend of hers, is there?'

Harry pursed his lips. 'Could have,' he remarked. 'I didn't think you'd know about him.'

Little smiled. 'Amazing what a boss knows about his staff. Without boasting I think I can say that the more the boss knows, the better he is. He can make them feel that he takes an interest in them, that he cares what happens to them and thinks of them as something more than machines to do the work.' He paused. 'You've told the police, of course?'

Harry nodded. 'To tell you the truth I thought that they may have been round here already.'

'We haven't seen anyone here,' Little said in answer to the implied question. 'Possibly they're short staffed and they'll get round some time this afternoon.'

Harry coughed. 'Seeing as you mentioned Tim,' he began, 'I'd like to ask you something.'

'What's that?'

Harry took his pipe out of his mouth, holding it by the stem, with two fingers.

'When I came in,' he said, 'there was a girl just going out. Who was she?'

'Why?'

'I went round to Tim's flat last night. She was there looking for him. I wondered if she might know anything that I don't, might be able to help in some way.'

174

'I see. Her name's Clare Roberts. I'll ask her to pop in for a minute if you want?'

The sun lit up one side of his face as he moved forward to a bell push on the desk.

'I don't want to cause — ' Harry began. He never finished the sentence.

Before Little's fingers touched the bell push there was a crash from the window. He flung up one hand, then slumped forward across the desk, knocking piles of paper to the floor. An ink bottle crashed, breaking, staining the carpet a deep blue colour.

Harry's eyes widened as he started forward.

Even he could see that Little was dead, shot through the temple.

★ ★ ★

At this moment, the car with Barbara and Baggott in it pulled up outside a house.

Baggott sat for a moment then got out, clicking the door shut softly, and went in to speak to Madge.

In one of the corridors at Scotland Yard, Chief Superintendent Peter Coates said:

'Going to be hot in here if this sun keeps up.'

The Inspector to whom he spoke grinned. 'That's progress, Pete. Switch the heating on in October and forget it. Never mind the weather. Can't even open the windows in this new building.'

Coates nodded gloomily. He was about to carry on to his office when the other man said:

'How's Sue?'

Sue was Coates' wife. She had been in bed with a heavy cold for three days. 'Not so bad now,' Coates replied. 'I was hoping to get home for dinner to look in but the Old Man's been chasing me most of the morning for a report about these paintings. Fifty thousand quid's worth of the stuff pinched from a lot of country houses. Could be the devil to track down, especially if they go out of the country.'

The Inspector nodded sympathetically. 'One of the penalties of promotion,' he said. 'That's what you get your fabulous salary for.'

He stood there grinning while Coates said: 'Not so much of the fabulous,' then turned as a messenger came up to them.

'Want me?' the Inspector asked.

'No, sir.' The man spoke with a Scottish accent. 'The Commander is asking for the Superintendent right away.'

'Hell!' Coates said. 'I can see that dinner getting further and further away.'

He hurried off, towards the Commander's office.

★   ★   ★

Twenty-five minutes later he was at Lennon's, with a small army of other men, photographers, fingerprint men, a doctor and various uniformed men from the Division. Several of the uniformed men went into the building opposite, from where the shot was reported to have come, while the various experts busied themselves in Little's office.

Coates stood by the desk. He was taller than any other man there, and most men in the force, but because of his spare body this size was not immediately apparent. He watched what was going on for a moment, nodded to himself and went out of the office.

The staff were sitting at their desks, the office buzzing with conversation. Above the general hum a girl's voice came shrilly.

'He wanted to see me but that man came instead!'

Another, deeper voice, said: 'It could have been you who was shot.'

Coates smiled grimly to himself and went out of the door. A room on the floor above had been taken over temporarily by the police, and it was in here that Harry Young had been asked to wait. Coates went up the stairs two at a time, glancing at his watch as he did so, realizing that it would be impossible to finish here and get home to Sue in time for lunch. It was his own fault for making the promise, of course; with the state of things at the Yard as they were at the moment, anyone was likely to be asked to do anything, all day and all night too if necessary. There was the missing doctor, too, and Harry Young's missing daughter. Unless this killing were the work of some lunatic there was a connection somewhere, which was why Coates, who had been directing the search for the other two in between doing the report, had been sent.

When he went into the room he found Harry sitting in one of the two chairs that had been brought in. He started to get up when Coates came in, but the Superintendent waved him back.

'Still feel shocked, Mr. Young?'

'I'm not so bad now, thank you.' Harry's voice was almost normal again. On the table in front of him was a cup of tea, very hot and very sweet, which he sipped from time to time.

Coates sat on the edge of the table, one leg swinging in the air. 'There's a doctor downstairs if you want him to give you something.'

'No thanks,' Harry smiled. 'I don't shock very easily, Superintendent. I'm feeling fine again now. Must admit that it was a bit of a shock at first, though. I mean, I was sitting right in front of him.'

Coates said: 'Take your time, Mr. Young, and tell me exactly what you saw.'

Harry took another sip of the tea, then sat back and thought for a moment before he gave his version of events. When he had finished Coates considered then asked:

'Did you see anyone who could have shot Mr. Little?'

'Not as far as I can remember. I could see the windows of the office block opposite, and I noticed that one of them around where the shot came from was open, but I didn't see anything other than that.'

'Was it open before the shooting?'

Harry pursed his lips. His hand went out for the tea, then stopped.

'Now you mention it,' he said, 'I don't think it was. There were two 'To Let' notices at first, and I'm sure that when I looked out after it had happened I could only see one. That would be the case if whoever shot him had opened a window, wouldn't it?'

'It would,' Coates agreed, swinging his leg. 'There was only one shot?'

Harry nodded.

'And did you move after it?'

'I can't remember.'

'Think carefully, Mr. Young, it could be important. Take your time, there's no hurry.'

Coates leaned back, the leg still swinging. He wanted to look at his watch, to see if there was any chance that he might be through with the routine in time to make a fleeting visit home, but to do it now would be a mistake, would give this man the impression that he was being hurried and would inevitably colour his answers in some way.

Harry took another sip of the tea.

'I don't think I did move,' he said finally. When he put the cup back his hand shook, and some of the tea slopped into the saucer.

'You're definite about that, sir?'

'Quite definite, yes.' Harry smiled. 'I don't react quickly to things these days and I suppose I was too shocked to move anyway.'

'I see.' To give himself time to think Coates pulled a packet of cigarettes from his pocket. He caught sight of a name on the packet, that of one of the firms with whom Lennon's didn't deal, and lit up quickly. That was an excuse, of course, that he smoked to give himself time to think. He smoked because he had to, even though Sue nagged him incessantly to stop, or at least to cut down. He drew the smoke into his lungs and said:

'I won't offer you one, Mr. Young. I can see you're a pipe man.'

'How — ' Harry broke off, realizing that he had stuffed his pipe into his jacket pocket and the stem was peeping out. 'Oh, yes. Wouldn't touch them things myself. They're gone too quickly.'

'You may be right.' Coates smiled, giving an impression of friendliness and warmth. 'On the other hand, they aren't as hard to light as a pipe. I don't think I could be bothered messing about like that before every smoke.'

Trivial things, but essential if Harry Young was to be put at ease again, and relaxed so that he would remember much more about the incident. The less tensed up he was, the more accurate would be the things that he did recall, too.

He pulled again at the cigarette.

Now he could look at his watch. It was almost half past eleven; with luck, there might still be time.

Almost subconsciously he began to go through the list of things to be done; there wouldn't be many people to see here, yet, as most of the search for clues would be concentrated on the building opposite. He would have to see the hall porter over there, of course, assuming there was one, and also the people on the floor concerned. Somehow he would have to find out who had keys to the offices that were empty, too, and go and see them.

He sighed.

An almost endless list of statements to be taken and checked, gone through for the slightest inconsistency.

Gone through, too, for any connection with this missing daughter business and the missing doctor.

That was likely to be the most difficult job, establishing a connection, however tenuous.

He said: 'Mr. Young, I'd like to talk to you about your daughter.'

'Ah, yes,' Harry answered. 'I thought you might have been round here sooner, actually.' It wasn't an accusation; merely a statement.

'We would have liked to have been,' Coates said, 'but the staff position isn't as good as it might be.'

'No, I realize that. What do you want to know about Barbara?'

'Is there anything that you can think of that connects her, Lennon's, the doctor and this boyfriend of hers? Anything, that is, apart from the obvious.'

'The obvious being that she's ran away with Tim Bocking?'

'That's right.'

'Superintendent, do you think that?' Harry asked the question bluntly.

Coates hesitated. 'I must admit that when I first heard of it, it looked pretty much that way,' he began, 'but the disappearance of Doctor Franklin put rather a different slant on things. So much so that I had an appeal put out, asking for information from anyone who'd seen him or his car. I was lucky; several people came forward and we were able to plot the route of his car after it had left your house, until he arrived at a house in a place called Speke Street.'

He paused.

'A neighbour says that the car was parked there for some time and then it was driven off and didn't come back. I could go to the house and ask one or two questions, but I've no proof and I don't want to blow the gaff prematurely, so I'm just having the house watched.'

He paused again, looking round for an ash tray, seeing one on a window sill and getting off the edge of the table to fetch it. He carried it over to the table again and perched himself where he had been before.

'All this is in confidence, of course, Mr. Young.'

'Of course.'

'I'm telling you because she is your daughter, after all, and I think you have a right to know what's going on.'

'Thank you.' Harry pulled on his pipe with two fingers, holding the bowl in the other hand, as if he were trying to stretch the stem. He did this twice then laid it in front of him on the table.

'And then there's Little's death,' Coates went on. 'Eloping couples don't shoot the boss. Of course, that could have been a mistake.'

'A mistake?' Harry looked startled.

'It goes back to what I said about the obvious. The killer may well have been aiming for Little; he could just as well have been aiming for you.'

★ ★ ★

For a moment there was silence in the small room, then Harry asked: 'For me?'

Coates nodded. 'That was why it was so important to know whether or not you moved after the incident. The fact that you didn't, and that the killer didn't try another shot, proves that theory wrong, I think. From what you've told me there was ample chance to shoot you at the time.'

'I never thought of that — '

'I shouldn't worry, Mr. Young. I'll have

a man to keep an eye on you if you want, but frankly I don't think you're in any danger.'

Harry nodded, his hands resting on his knees. Suddenly he said: 'There is a connection, you know. I can't see how it fits in, but you might be able to.'

'What's that?' Coates was suddenly alert.

'A girl. She was at Tim Bocking's flat last night, and then I saw her here, in Little's office, just before I went in. In fact we met in the doorway.'

'Did you, indeed. Any idea of her name?'

'I asked Mr. Little that. Clare Roberts, he said.'

'I'll have a word with her,' Coates said, standing up. 'I don't think there's anything else — ' He broke off. 'Yes there is, just one other thing. Do you know where Tim Bocking works?'

'I've no idea,' Young said. 'Barbara did mention it, but I've completely forgotten.'

Coates nodded. 'I dare say we can find out some other way. Right, Mr. Young, I'll have some copies of your statement for you to sign. I'll send someone round to your house when they're ready. In the meantime, I'll have a word with Clare Roberts.'

* * *

The building had been sealed off, and everyone prevented from entering or leaving. The fact that Clare Roberts was nowhere to be found was significant; it meant that she had gone out before the police arrived, and that she might have a good reason for wanting to avoid them.

14

When Coates returned to Little's office, he found policemen still in control of the office itself, and panic and excitement still in the outer office. The shrill voiced girl who had been shouting before was silent now, listening to someone else, a tall, thin young man, speaking in a deep voice.

Coates went past them and into Little's office.

A constable on the door said: 'The doctor's had the body taken away, sir. I think the fingerprint people have almost finished, too.'

'Good.' Coates looked round the room. Apart from the shattered window, the ink stain on the carpet and a dark stain on the desk that was blood but could have been anything, there were very few signs that anything had happened in the room. Certainly there was nothing to indicate that murder had been committed here.

He wondered again about Clare Roberts. No one seemed to have seen her go out. She certainly hadn't gone out after the police had arrived, when everyone had been stopped from either entering or leaving; that fact in itself was suspicious, without the knowledge that she was connected with Tim Bocking in some way. He wondered if there would be anyone here who would know anything about her. The firm would have her address, but there would be nothing in their records to show who her friends were, what she did in her spare time, how she was involved with Bocking, or any of a dozen other things that he wanted to know.

He turned back to the constable.

'I'll be in the outer office for some time if anyone wants me.'

'Very good, sir.'

As he came out into the other, larger office, and gazed round, the buzz of conversation stopped, almost as if everyone knew that he wanted some information from them. His eyes travelled slowly until he saw the girl who had been talking before; she seemed the type who knew everyone, and there was a chance that she might know Clare Roberts.

He said: 'Would you mind if I just had a word with you.'

She stood up, slowly. She was only young, about the same age as the girl who had first vanished, he reckoned, smartly dressed in a short green skirt in the latest style and a lace ruffled white blouse. She looked puzzled, now, as if trying to guess what she could tell him that he didn't already know from someone else. As she stepped out from behind her desk Coates heard a soft movement from behind.

He looked round.

A man stood there, a file of papers in one hand. 'Excuse me,' he said, 'but will you be long here?'

'Some time yet, I'm afraid.'

The man ran a hand over his forehead. 'What a mess!' he said wearily. 'There'll be no chance of calming them down for ages yet.'

'I can see that,' Coates said shortly. 'A murder does tend to upset routine.'

The man waved one arm in the air. 'Don't get me wrong,' he said earnestly. 'I'm not complaining. I'm just wondering how I can best restore order in the office.'

'Let it die down itself. It will if you give it another half-hour or so. I can tell the difference now from how they were when I first came. It's always the same; I shouldn't worry.'

He paused.

The girl stood nearby, obviously listening.

Coates said: 'No objection to my asking questions of your staff, is there?'

'No, none at all. Go ahead.'

'Thanks.' Coates turned to the girl. 'Do you know Clare Roberts?'

'Yes,' she answered at once, all the shrillness gone from her voice now that she didn't have to shout to make herself heard. 'She worked in this office.'

'If I asked you one or two questions about her, do you think you could tell me?'

'About Clare?' The shrillness was back again.

'That's right.'

'But she couldn't — ' She broke off.

'I didn't say she had. Just answer what I asked you.'

'Well, yes, I think so.' The girl seemed even more puzzled than she had been before.

'Good. We've got a room upstairs which is better than here. Come with me.'

He led the way to the room where he had seen Harry Young, who had now left. The girl, who told him that her name was Yvonne Fletcher sat in the chair that Young had used, while Coates perched himself on the table again.

'Now, Yvonne,' he began, 'I'd like to see Clare but she doesn't seem to be here. Have you any idea where she might be?'

'None at all. She acted as confidential secretary for Mr. Little, and when she came out of his office before — ' She stopped, her hand going to her mouth. 'That's it,' she said, a tone of relief in her voice. 'You want to see her because she was in there just before it happened.'

'That's right,' Coates agreed. 'Go on with what you were saying.'

'Well, she went in to take some letters,

like she does every morning about that time. When she came out she put her notebook on her desk, went to get her coat and went out. She didn't speak to anyone, but it isn't unusual for her to go out like that; Mr. Little often asked her to go errands for him.'

'I see,' Coates mused. 'So she could be back anytime.'

'Oh yes. She used to bring sandwiches for lunch, so she's certain to be back for lunch time.'

'What time's that?'

'For her, any time now.' Yvonne glanced at her watch. 'About ten minutes.'

Coates nodded. He could wait that long if there was a chance of her coming back.

'Do you know anything about what she did outside work?' he asked.

'You mean boyfriends, that sort of thing?'

'Yes.'

'As it happens, I do.' Yvonne laughed. 'There was a bit of an upset about it a couple of months ago when it came out that she was after the same boy as Barbara Young.'

She paused.

'His name was Tim Bocking.' She looked at him narrowly. 'Isn't it funny that both Clare and Barbara seem to have disappeared?'

★ ★ ★

By half past twelve, Clare Roberts had still not returned.

By twelve thirty-five a call had gone out to all Divisions.

Find her.

★ ★ ★

Coates went back to speak to the constable in Little's office, the one of the many who had been in there who was still there.

'I think we should be all right here, now,' he said. 'Know where Sergeant Hopkins is?'

'He's across the road, sir, in the other office block.'

'Thank you.'

He turned abruptly and hurried out of the building. As he tried to cross the road

195

a small man wearing glasses tried to stop him.

'Anything for me, Super?'

'Not yet. When there is anything for the press I'll let you know.'

'Aye, and every other reporter, too,' retorted the man, his Scottish accent coming over strongly. 'Can't you even give me his name?'

'Who's name?'

'The man who's been killed.'

'Who said anyone had been killed?' Coates asked blandly, and hurried across the road.

A constable standing by a police car stopped him. 'There's just been a call for you, sir. Like to use my radio?'

'Thanks.' Coates slid into the car and called the Yard. If this was a message about Clare Roberts it was quicker than he had expected, quicker than anything he had ever known.

The message was not about Clare. What he heard caused him to compress his lips and then go into the building in search of Sergeant Hopkins.

'Found anything?'

'Not much yet, sir. The lock has been forced on one of the empty offices. Only one though; looks as if someone knew which was the window to shoot at.'

'Obviously. Hoppy, those men we had on that house in Speke Street, where Franklin's car was parked last night, have loused things up. Two men have come out of the house, separately, and walked to the Market Hall. One of them got into a car there and was lost. They're still watching the other one. The house itself is apparently empty.'

Hopkins was about to speak when the constable who had spoken before came in.

'Another call for you, sir.'

This time the message was brief and to the point.

'We've found a body. The description tallies with that of Doctor Maurice Franklin.'

15

Speke Street was almost deserted when Coates reached it. He had left Hopkins in charge at Lennon's, and was alone in the police car. That didn't really matter, as one of the Divisional men who had been watching the house would be there waiting for him. As the car stopped, he hurried over to it.

Brushing aside the man's apologies for losing the men from the house, Coates asked: 'Which house is it?'

'That one, sir.'

'Any sign that they may be coming back?'

'Not so far.'

'Hm.'

Coates inspected the house, not liking what he saw. All the houses in the street were the same; all had bay windows, most had attics, most of them were in reasonable repair. This one was easily the worst of the lot, probably rented under a false name, to make things harder.

'Anyone else shown any interest in the house?'

'No, sir.'

Coates considered quickly. He had no warrant, but there was ample excuse for going into the house. The fact that the men had more or less fled after being visited by the police was enough for that, especially since it was also the last place where Franklin had been seen alive.

He said: 'Come with me.'

The two men went up to the front door of the house, where Coates bent to look at the lock. When he saw that it would be quite simple to force he said softly: 'We're going in.'

Soon, the door was open, with only minor damage.

Coates went in first. There was always a chance that someone might be in, even though there had been no answer before, and that someone, if he were a killer, could have a gun.

Nothing moved in the house.

The constable said: 'What do you make of that, sir?' pointing to the side of the corridor near the end furthest from the door, where there were scuff marks in the dust.

Coates went over to them.

'Looks like something was laid down there.'

'Possibly a body.'

'Could be. Could have been the doctor after he was killed, but let's have a look round before we jump to conclusions.'

He went into the first room, saw the phone on the table and immediately realized the possibilities of fingerprints on it. He turned to the constable.

'Go outside to my car and get on to the Yard. Tell them I want a photographer and fingerprint man here as soon as possible.'

'Yes, sir.' The man hurried out.

Coates left the room. There was little point in touching anything, just in case there were prints that might be of some use. It was unlikely, of course, as unlikely as the fact that the men who had rented the house had done so under their real names, but it was just possible. If, as he was hoping, the policeman's visit had panicked them, then there was a chance that they had forgotten some simple thing.

The constable returned.

'They're on their way.'

'Good. Let's have a look round, but try not to disturb too much.'

The two men went out into the passage again, and then into the other room, where there were stairs. The constable stayed at the foot, while Coates climbed them slowly, alert for anything that might be a warning of a desperate man up there.

He saw the half open bedroom door, and the furniture pressed against it.

He didn't want to push the door any more, fearful of disturbing something before there were pictures of it as it had been found. He returned to the other man.

'This type of house always has a cellar. Must be that other door off the passage. I suggest that we go and have a look round there.'

There was more chance of finding something there, he thought, than in the normal rooms of the house, though to judge from what he had seen of the bedroom, someone had been held prisoner there recently. The position of the furniture was against this; it looked as if it might have been more to keep someone out than someone in.

He was musing along these lines when he reached the door that led into the corridor. He stopped, his hand on the edge of the door.

Someone was creeping along the passage.

* * *

Coates moved as far as he could to the door, opening it a little further, until to move any more would have warned the man outside.

The footsteps continued.

The man might have a gun.

Coates turned to see where the constable was. As he did so, he saw him turn towards the door, his mouth open to speak. Desperately, he waved his hand for silence.

The constable paused.

The footsteps came nearer, very slowly, very steady.

Very near the door.

When he judged that the man was almost on the point of opening the door, Coates sprang out. He saw a dark shape immediately in front of him, moving back sharply. Reacting quickly, he reached out his hand, caught the man's lapel and dragged him back.

'All right,' he said. 'What do you want?'

The man he held, a burly, florid-faced man, struggled to free himself. 'I might ask you the same question,' he said gruffly.

'What do you mean?'

The burly man didn't answer. Instead, he tried to break the grasp on his lapel, then suddenly jerked his leg up sharply. The blow landed on Coates' shin, making him cry out and loose his hold. The burly man was free now, but, incredibly, was making no attempt to get away.

He said: 'I don't know who the devil you are, but — '

Coates took his warrant card from his pocket and held it out.

'Police?' the big man asked warily.

'That's right.'

'Have you any kind of warrant for being in here?'

'I can soon get one.' Coates spoke grimly. The constable was by his side, his eyes bright, watching the burly man carefully, as if he thought that his attitude was part of some trickery.

'But you haven't got one at the moment?' The man persisted with his questioning.

'No, sir.' Coates seemed to pause. 'Are you the owner of this house, or any other connection with it?'

'I own it but I don't live here. That isn't the point — '

'It may not be to you, sir, but it is to me,' Coates interrupted. 'There is more than a possibility that murder was committed here last night. Who were the tenants here?'

'A murder?'

'Who was living here?'

The burly man hesitated, then reached for one of the doors. 'We can talk better in here.'

'I'd rather you didn't touch anything,' Coates told him. 'We can say all that has to be said while we're standing here.'

The burly man laughed, much less sure of himself now than he had been when he had come in. 'Fingerprints, of course. The house was rented to a man named Jenkins, but in view of what you've said that is likely to be a false name.'

'Know anything about him?'

'Not very much. He'll have written the usual letter of application, of course. All prospective tenants have to do that.'

'What did he look like?'

The burly man pursed his lips. 'Pretty ordinary looking really. About the only thing you'd notice would be his face. He always reminded me of a clown.'

'You can't give me a better description than that?' Coates asked.

'I didn't really see very much of him,' the landlord said. 'I only came here once a week to collect the rent. Sometimes I saw an American here, too, but I know nothing at all about him other than that the other man called him Tex.'

'Tex,' Coates mused. He turned to the

constable. 'Mean anything to you? He was in your patch.'

'Not very much, sir.' The constable reddened slightly.

'Can't really expect it to.' Coates paused again and the landlord asked:

'It's not my tenant who's been killed, is it?'

'No.' Abruptly Coates turned. After telling the constable to take the landlord's name and address he went down into the cellar. Once he reached the bottom of the steps he found the light dimmed considerably, and as he felt around for a switch he heard the burly man shout:

'It's on your right, about two feet from the cellar door.'

Coates went forward, his right hand brushing lightly against the wall. He found the switch, pressed it down and blinked for a moment in the sudden light. His eyes drifted round the room. From where he was standing he couldn't see beyond the pillar which jutted out, but he could see the bed, rumpled as if someone had slept in it, and part of a dark, irregular stain on the floor. With a low grunt of satisfaction he started forward, bending down to examine it. As far as he could tell it was blood; a proper examination could wait until the men from the Yard arrived.

He could see round the pillar now; he saw the coal and wood scattered below the grating, but attached no significance to them.

The bed was more interesting. On it, half hidden beneath the blankets, he found a girl's coat, which fitted Harry Young's description of what his daughter had been wearing. On the floor by the foot of the bed was a glass jug, and a small glass with about half an inch of water in it. These he carefully left untouched, while he fingered the two bits of cord attached to the old-fashioned headboard.

He heard a sound at the top of the steps.

The constable called: 'The men from the Yard are here now, sir.'

Coates straightened. 'I'll be right up.'

Half-way up the steps he met the photographer, an old friend of his.

207

'What have you got for me now?' the photographer asked, a smile on his face.

'Quite a bit. If you get down there you'll find out what there is.'

As the photographer went on into the cellar, a tall, chubby man standing at the top of the steps called:

'Any fingerprints you want doing first, Superintendent?'

'I'm not sure what you'll find.' Coates reached the top of the steps and stood alongside the man; although they were both the same height, Coates in fact looked smaller. 'There are a lot of things that look promising but they've probably all been wiped. I'd like you down in the cellar, but give Whitie a chance first. In the meantime, there's a phone in that room there which had been used recently and a door which has been broken down and could be full of prints. See what you can do for me, will you, I've a couple of calls to make.'

He turned and went towards the front door. The constable was on the steps, moving on a small knot of onlookers attracted by the two police cars outside the house; Coates waited until they had reluctantly drifted away before asking for the landlord's address.

The man took out his notebook. 'There you are, sir.' He smiled almost smugly as he put his hand back into his pocket and took out something long and thin, wrapped in a handkerchief. 'Just in case there is anything fishy there'll probably be one or two prints on this pen he used.'

Coates took the pen, putting it into his pocket, nodding his thanks. It was unlikely that the man's prints would be needed, but not impossible, but in any case it showed initiative on the part of the constable.

'What's your name?'

'Haynes, sir.'

He nodded; at some time he would arrange for Haynes' superior to have a word of encouragement with him.

The landlord's office was quite near. After a glance at his watch Coates got into his car and drove off.

★　★　★

The letter signed 'R. Jenkins' was simple and not of much use except for one thing. There was an address on it, and there was just a faint chance that something might be known of him there.

★ ★ ★

A small, blonde, middle-aged lady at the other address laughed, and rubbed flour coated hands on a striped apron when Coates mentioned the name Jenkins.

'Jenkins?' she said. 'We've lived here these twenty years and there's never been anyone of that name here in that time.'

★ ★ ★

Coates went back to the house in Speke Street, where he reckoned that the others would be nearly finished. He was right; they were waiting for him in the hall when he went in.

'Found anything?' he asked.

'A little. Peter's got most of it,' the photographer answered.

'Phone's clean,' the other man announced.

'All the doors and woodwork have been wiped down, there's only a few smudges on them, no use at all. The jug downstairs has a half a thumbprint on it, but there's nearly a full set from one hand on the glass.' He shook his head gloomily. 'Those'll be the person who drank from it, probably the girl. Apart from that, and the coat, there's this which you missed.'

He took something wrapped in white cloth from his pocket.

'What is it?'

'A shoe. A girl's shoe; that we found under the bed.'

'Any prints?'

'One or two. They look as if they'll match the glass.'

Coates went outside and got back into his car. Unless some of the prints on the glass turned out not to belong to the girl, they had no way of tracing the people who had rented the house. The name Jenkins was certainly false, though he would have someone look in Records, just in case.

He wasn't optimistic.

16

About four miles from the house at Speke Street was another house, completely unlike the first one. This was a detached house, about as large as two of the Speke Street houses knocked together, and was very modern and up to date. It had four bedrooms; in the smallest of these was Barbara Young.

She lay very still, only semi-conscious, pain streaking through her head every time she moved.

* * *

In one of the downstairs rooms, Baggott-known-as-Jenkins stood by the big bay window which was so different from the one he had known at Speke Street.

'He shouldn't be as late as this,' he muttered.

'Stop worrying.' The woman who sat in a chair behind him stood up and joined him at the window. 'He's probably having a bit of trouble with the police.'

Baggott turned savagely to face her. 'That's just what does worry me,' he said loudly.

'Well, don't let it.' The woman's voice was soothing, obviously in an attempt to calm Baggott before he flew into one of his rages. 'He'll have more sense than to bring them here.'

'That isn't the point.' Baggott went over to the chair where the woman had been sitting and flopped down in it. 'That isn't the point at all. If the cops are following Tex, he'll think I've double-crossed him somehow.' His voice rose. 'You know what he'll do if he thinks that, Madge! He'll kill me!'

★ ★ ★

Upstairs, Barbara heard this as a faint echoing voice. She was nearly conscious again, now, aware of the pain in her head, and of the cords at her wrists and ankles. The gag was tight at her mouth, too, and she lay on one side, which was numb with cramp. Apart from the pain in her head, there seemed to be no other injuries, and even though her mind was so slow and sluggish, the events since she had left the other house stood out with startling clarity.

Her father.

She had seen her father walking along the pavement; if she had been allowed to stay at the window for another few seconds he would have seen her, too, and she would probably be free now. As it was, she was in another house, and this time there was little hope of the police tracing it.

She tossed on the bed, trying to free herself, but she was bound so tightly that the ropes cut into the flesh.

Thinking of her father brought her mother back to mind. What was she doing in hospital? Was she seriously ill? Was it something to do with the fact that she, Barbara, had vanished? She had never known her mother ill enough to warrant going to hospital before; there must be a connection.

She tried to put that from her mind,

and concentrate on getting away.

The room she was in was sparsely furnished, almost like the one she had barricaded herself in at the other place, but somehow she sensed that this was a completely different kind of house. There was a carpet on the floor, for one thing, which there hadn't been at the other house; for another, there were flowers at the window, a vase of yellow daffodils.

Flowers!

At a time like this!

She realized that that must mean a woman lived in the house, and remembered Madge, whom she hoped to win round to her side. She was certain that if she was once allowed to speak to the woman alone, she could do it, but the trouble was that this situation wouldn't arise. If there was the slightest chance of weakness on the woman's part, Baggott or the American would make sure that they were never alone.

She was afraid that the men would come to torture her soon.

What could she tell them, what could she do to make them understand that she didn't know anything about what they wanted to know, what could she do to stop them?

Memory of the knife that the American had held so near her came back, and she gasped as she thought of it cutting into her flesh. There must be a way out.

There *had* to be a way out.

★   ★   ★

It was some time later when she heard the footsteps on the stairs. She cringed back, fearing that this was Baggott or the American, but realized then that the steps were too light.

They were a woman's steps.

This must be Madge, the woman who would be the only one who might help her.

If there was only one set of footsteps, that must mean she was coming in on her own.

Barbara lay back on the bed. The door opened and the woman came in, carrying a tray, which she placed on something out of Barbara's line of vision, before dragging a small table over to the bed.

Barbara saw her, then.

She recognized the woman who had originally kidnapped her.

Madge put the tray on the table and leaned over her. 'If you promise not to struggle I'll untie you. Nod your head if you agree.'

Barbara nodded, and Madge took out a short knife. She cut through the cords, and Barbara moved her arms stiffly. For a moment nothing happened, but then cramp raced through them, until the pain made her sob and cry into the gag.

Gradually, the pain faded.

'Are you going to shout if I take the gag off?' the woman asked.

Barbara shook her head.

'You'd better keep your mouth shut, too, or I'll know what to do with you.' Again the knife, followed by faint cramp in her lips, and a feeling of dry emptiness in her mouth.

Madge had brought a tray of food, the first she had eaten since she had been kidnapped.

She lifted it on to the bed, placing it

over Barbara's legs, warning her to keep still so that it wouldn't spill.

Barbara nodded, not trusting herself to speak until she had drunk some of the tea that was on the tray. She took a small sip, letting the fluid stay in her mouth for as long as she could. It made even the pain in her head feel much better; she took another sip and the dry, evil taste that had been there for so long was gone completely.

Now she could start on the food. Chips, a fried egg and some pieces of bacon, fatter than she usually liked it, but she had not eaten for so long that she didn't care. She gulped the food down, while the woman sat on the edge of the bed, the knife in her hand. When she had finished, Barbara said to her:

'Please, you must help me!'

Madge shook her head.

'But — '

Madge stood up. 'I'm not helping you,' she stated flatly. 'Put your wrists together so that I can bind you again.'

Tears pricked at Barbara's eyes. 'I don't know how you can do it,' she said softly.

'How can you sit there and see another woman treated like this, kept here to be tortured by those two men.' She ignored the hard glitter in Madge's eye and went on: 'I don't even know what they want to know! How can I make them believe that?'

Madge put her face very close to hers. 'Listen, kid, if it would help to find Tim Bocking I'd sit here and torture you myself. You get no help from me.'

Her tone was flat and final, and she emphasized each word.

Barbara said: 'You ought to be ashamed.'

'Perhaps I should. Now do what I told you, and don't try any funny stuff or I'll hit you so hard that you won't move again for a long time.'

Barbara lay still while the woman bound and gagged her again, then watched her collect the tray and leave the room. The closing of the door was sharp and final, and meant only one thing.

There was going to be no help from anyone.

★ ★ ★

Some miles away, Tex drove skilfully and fast. He had always driven, and when he had been in the Market Centre he had been glad that a hire car was arranged and waiting for him a few blocks away. He had stayed at the stall for a minute or two too long, and when he had looked round it had been to see the two plain clothes men who had been watching Speke Street standing very near to him.

He had moved quickly, shouldering aside a fat woman carrying two bulging shopping bags, picking up a small boy and whirling him to one side.

The policemen had followed.

Tex had been almost running now. The men were pushing their way through the crowd, but the American was first, and the detectives were catching much of the crowd's anger at being pushed like this.

By the time he reached the car they were some distance away.

He had driven off, sure that he was safe. It wasn't until a couple of minutes later that he had realized he was being followed. He couldn't go back to Speke Street now, or to Madge's. The only thing to do was head out of London and shake them off.

He thought now that he had succeeded, and his mind turned back to Barbara.

She appealed to him, and unlike Baggott he didn't particularly want to kill her. She had done them no harm, she knew little enough about them, and she couldn't tell the police anything that they didn't already know. Her only value really was that she knew where Bocking was; when she had told them that, Baggott would insist that she died.

Why add to the killing that had been done already?

It only encouraged the police to come a little closer.

He accelerated past a lorry and glanced at his watch. He would have to get back to the house soon, or Baggott would start to panic.

He increased speed slightly.

★ ★ ★

Back at the house, Baggott stood by the window again. He turned when he heard a sound behind him, and saw Madge.

'Well?' she asked.

'Well, what?'

'Where is he?'

'How do I know?' Baggott walked slowly away from the window, to the chair he had used before. 'He's probably been pinched by the cops. He'll give the lot of us away yet.'

'Not if I know Tex.' Madge spoke sharply. 'If the cops have got him, he won't say a word, you can be sure of that.'

Baggott grunted. Madge went across to the window herself. Outside, a group of children were playing with a bike, taking it in turns to ride it, a dog was running up and down, barking, and two women were pushing prams slowly, gossiping as they walked.

There was no sign of Tex.

One of the children fell off the bike, and was surrounded by the rest, one of whom ignored the child and concentrated entirely on the bike.

Madge turned back to Baggott. 'It doesn't look as if he's coming, Baggott boy.'

'Don't call me that!'

'Sorry.' She sat down in the chair next to his and drew her legs up on to it. For a while neither of them spoke, then Baggott broke the silence.

'Where the hell is he?'

The peal of the doorbell cut across his words.

Madge stood up, moving towards the door. 'Here he is now.' She went through the hall, opened the front door and looked at the stranger who stood there, raising his hat politely.

He said: 'Good afternoon. I'm Superintendent Coates from the Yard. I'm looking for Miss Little. Miss Madge Little.'

17

This was the type of job which Coates never liked. In addition, to make things worse, he had been delayed at the Yard, by the urgent need to arrange appeals for information regarding Bocking and the girl, Clare Roberts. In particular, they wanted to know where Bocking worked; the only person who might be able to help them in this, Harry Young, had no idea.

At length, everything was arranged, and Coates left to go and see the next of kin of the dead man, Little.

'May I come in?' he asked.

'Of course.' The woman held the door open, almost mechanically, he thought.

He said: 'Are you Miss Little?'

'I am.' Now the voice held suspicion.

'I'm afraid I've some bad news for you, Miss Little.' He paused fractionally then hurried on. 'Your brother, who works at Lennon's, was shot this morning. I'm afraid he's dead.'

The woman gasped. The corners of her mouth dropped and her eyes widened, and she reached out one hand to grasp the back of a nearby chair.

'Shot?'

'I'm afraid so. Is there anyone you'd like me to contact?'

'No. No, I — ' She broke off. 'I — '

'Take it easy, Miss Little.' Coates pulled up one of the other chairs, noting almost subconsciously that even though the woman seemed to be alone in the house, two of the chairs had been sat in recently. The woman sat down and passed a hand over her forehead.

'Do you know who shot him?' she demanded suddenly.

'I'm afraid not — yet.'

'You hope to?'

Coates nodded.

'I see.' The woman's voice, which had been strong when she had been asking the questions, faded now until he could hardly hear it.

'Miss Little, do you feel up to answering one or two questions? If you don't, say so and I'll leave them, but your answers could help us to catch the man quickly.'

'Must you ask them now?'

'I know how you must feel,' answered the superintendent, 'but the trouble is that, as you know, there's no one else I can ask, and anything that you tell me may help me in my investigations.'

'Yes, yes, of course.' The woman's voice was still faint. 'Actually, Johnny and I were never as close as all that, I don't know why. Perhaps it was because we never had much in common.'

'I see. How often did you see him, Miss Little?'

'Hardly at all.' Now her voice was stronger, much stronger. She felt around on the seat of the chair until she found a packet of cigarettes, shook one out and lit it with a hand that trembled only slightly. She hesitated, then offered the packet to Coates.

'Are you allowed to, on duty?'

'I am, but not at the moment,' Coates answered, then let her wait for a few seconds before he spoke again.

'What do you call seeing him hardly at all?'

'Only about every two or three months.'

Coates nodded. At least that explained why she had taken the news so calmly. He was still speculating idly about the two chairs, but he didn't think it important enough to delve into it deeply.

'How long had your brother worked for Lennon's?'

'Not very long actually.'

'You sound as if I should be surprised at that.' Coates smiled, in an attempt to ease the atmosphere.

'Do I?' The woman drew on the cigarette, then blew out a cloud of smoke before continuing. 'I suppose it's because the sort of job he had is the kind that makes you think of people who've been there for years. He'd only been there about four or five years.'

'He started there with that job?'

'I think so. It's very difficult to recall what was going on then.'

Coates nodded non-committally. 'Did you see a lot of your brother at any time in the past?'

'Not really. We've never been a close family, Superintendent. It may come as a surprise to you that I hardly know what's happening to my closest relation, but — '

'Not at all.' Coates' voice was affable. It had taken a lot of questions and looking up of records at Lennon's to establish that this woman was next of kin. Little had been unmarried; everyone there knew that much, but no one seemed to know any more.

He said: 'What I'm after, Miss Little, is whether you know of anything in his life, either recently or in the past, that could have provided a motive for this murder?'

The woman thought, putting both hands on the arms of the chair and letting the cigarette hang from her lips until the ash threatened to drop over her dress. She tapped it into a handily placed ashtray, using quick, jerky motions.

'I can't think of anything,' she said at last.

'Nothing at all?'

'Nothing at all, Superintendent.'

Coates pressed his lips together. That was the curious feature about this killing.

It was so peculiarly motiveless, almost like that of the doctor, yet the killer had obviously taken the trouble to get everything right. The only solution other than some hidden motive was that he had been after Harry Young, and had got the wrong man.

But there seemed to be no motive there, either.

And if he had been after Young, why hadn't he taken a second shot while the man had been sitting motionless after the shooting?

He must have been after Little. But there was no motive. Correction: there was no obvious motive. He had been relying on this woman to provide him with something, anything which he could use as a lead, but she had failed; only now did he realize just how much he had been relying on her.

He tried another course.

'Did your brother have a lot of activities out of work?'

His smile might have meant something.

She said: 'I'm afraid I know very little about him. He could have stayed in his house every evening or he could have been out with a typist, for all I know. Every time I went round he was in, but that doesn't tell you anything because we always arranged visits like that beforehand.'

Coates said: 'No it isn't much help, is it.'

Madge Little smiled. 'Have you reached a blank wall now, Superintendent, or is there some other line you can try?'

'I'm not sure yet. It may fit in with another case that I'm investigating, I'll have to see how it goes.' He stood up. 'I'll leave you in peace now, anyway. If there are any more questions, I take it that you'll have no objections to answering them?'

'None at all, Superintendent, just come and ask.' Her cigarette had burned down almost to the filter; she stubbed it out as she stood up.

'Thank you.' Coates stepped through the door as she opened it. 'I'll do my best to get the killer for you.'

He left, walking quickly to his car, noticing that the woman watched him from the window. As he opened the car door, he heard the radio crackle. The message was not for him, and he drove off slowly, uncertain whether to go back to the Yard or whether to go and see Harry Young. In a way he would have liked to go through everything in the case again, starting with Lil Benson, who had first reported that the doctor was missing, and taking in the Young's, Lennon's and Tim Bocking's flat.

He would have liked to know where Bocking worked, too.

The radio crackled again.

'A message for Superintendent Coates.'

He answered it, and heard the voice of Sergeant Hopkins.

'I've had the bullet that killed Little checked with the one that killed Doctor Franklin, sir.'

'Well?'

Hopkins voice faded slightly with the atmospherics, then came through strongly.

'They're not the same, sir.'

* * *

At this moment, back at Madge Little's house, Baggott was sitting in the chair that Madge had just left.

'I tell you,' he said hoarsely, 'I've no idea who killed Johnny. It could have been Tex, I suppose, but I don't think so.'

He looked up at her, and his face was sagging.

'Madge. I don't like it. What the hell's going on?'

18

Commander Howard-Jones of the C.I.D. looked at Coates across his wide desk.

'Well, Superintendent, how are we doing on this double murder case?'

'Not too well, sir.' Coates spent a moment gazing round the large, airy office, much bigger than his own. 'In fact, all the leads or clues that we have seem to have dried up. The three people who could help us most seem to have vanished.'

'That's Bocking, Barbara Young and Clare Roberts?' put in Howard-Jones.

'That's right, sir.'

'Think any of them are guilty in any way? Think that's why they've disappeared? What about the Young girl, for instance, she was the first?'

'I don't think she's guilty. We found her coat and shoes at the house in Speke Street, and signs that someone had been tied to the bed there. We can only

233

suppose it was her. As for the others,' he spread his hands, 'they could be connected in any way, but I've no idea which is the right one.'

'And what have you done to find out?'

Howard-Jones' voice was very precise. There were those at the Yard who said that he was only out to find fault, and that the frequent conferences which had been a result of his promotion earlier in the previous year were held only so that he could point out things which hadn't been done, or which he thought had been done wrongly. Coates was not so sure; he knew that Howard-Jones was an enthusiast, and that he was anxious to see the C.I.D. with a hundred per cent success rate. It was true, also, that since he had been made Commander the number of crimes solved had begun to rise slightly.

Coates said: 'When the men fled from Speke Street, and it became obvious that the house had been rented under a false name, I arranged for everyone living in the street and in the adjoining streets, to be interviewed. I don't know if you know the area, sir, but there are quite a number

234

of back streets around there. Certain to be one or two people who make a point of knowing everyone else's business. We might pick up something.'

'It'll be a long job.'

'I know that, sir, but there's little else I can do. I have arranged for photos of the girls and the doctor to go in the papers and on the T.V. news, with a request for information, and I've put out Bocking's description. There aren't any photos of him, so I've had something done on the Identikit.'

'And so far there are no results?'

'There hasn't really been time for much. The noon editions are out, but they only carry Bocking's picture.'

Howard-Jones remained silent for a moment and then asked what information Bocking's employers had been able to give.

'That's part of the trouble, sir. We don't know who they are. Harry Young is the only man who could help us there, and he never listened when his daughter was telling him. I've had a call out on the news for them to get in touch with us since mid-morning but there hasn't been any reply yet.'

'There could be a good reason,' Howard-Jones mused. 'On the other hand, it could be that they themselves are involved in this.'

'Could be,' Coates agreed cautiously.

'Of course it could.' The Commander leaned back. 'If they haven't responded by tomorrow we must try to get Young to remember the name. There must be a point in this silence. I think that if we can find them we'll be a long way towards breaking this.'

He gave a nod of dismissal.

Coates went out. Somehow, he *had* to find out where Bocking worked.

* * *

The flat where Tim Bocking lived was silent and locked when Coates and Sergeant Hopkins reached it, but a key had been provided by the owners. Coates had snatched a quick meal, and had a brief word with Sue over the phone, before leaving to look at all angles of the case again. Doctor Franklin's surgery he had found in the hands of John Benson, Lil Benson's nephew, a tall good-looking lad of about twenty-five or six, who had spent longer than was strictly necessary in looking at the picture of Barbara that he had been shown, before saying that he had never seen her.

He was taking the surgery as well as he could, he explained, while working out his notice at the hospital where he worked now.

'You're leaving?' Coates enquired.

'Yes.' Benson smiled. 'Actually, Mr. Franklin left me the practice in his will. I only found out by chance, when Aunt Lil asked me to try to keep things going for a few days.'

After leaving there, they had gone to Bocking's flat. This was one place where, owing to shortage of men, a thorough search hadn't been carried out; with things developing the way they were, this was now considered an essential, and Coates slipped the key into the door and turned it.

The lock clicked back easily, as though it had been well oiled at some time.

The front door opened directly on to a small living-room. Two doors opened off this. Through one of them, which was half open, Coates could see the edge of a cooker, and some empty tins in a pile on the floor. The other one was closed, and obviously led to the bedroom.

Hopkins said: 'Shall I start in there?'

'Just let me have a look round first.' Coates stepped across to the bedroom door and opened it.

He didn't see the girl until he was well into the room. She lay on her back across the narrow bed, one arm flung out and the other at her side, the fingers bent as if she had been trying to claw at something. One of her own stockings was wound tightly round and round her throat.

Obviously she was dead.

She fitted the description of Clare Roberts.

★ ★ ★

238

Barbara Young knew nothing of this as she too lay on a bed. She was concerned only with how she could free herself by her own efforts, having realized that no one else was going to help her. What seemed like hours of trying to undo the ropes that bound her had proved fruitless; there must be something else that she could do.

She moved slightly, trying to ease the cramp in her limbs.

She saw the window, and an idea came.

If she could get off the bed, crawl across to the window and break it with her feet, she might be able to use the sharp edges of the glass as a knife. In addition, someone outside might hear the sound of the glass as it shattered, and, on seeing what was going on, would almost certainly call the police.

She wriggled, trying to get off the bed without falling and alerting the people downstairs.

She managed to roll over on to her side, and then to swing her legs forward so that they hung over the edge of the bed.

Another roll brought her almost to the edge, so that she had only to lever herself up with her elbows to be sitting there. She did this, then paused, wondering how best to get across to the window. The best hope, she realized, lay in keeping on her feet, crossing the room with little jumps, then sitting before the window and breaking it with her feet. There was a risk that she might hurt herself, but it was better than lying there, just waiting for Baggott to come back.

She eased herself off the bed, more anxious now than she had been at any time during her imprisonment, and she knew that this would be her last chance to escape.

Pain streaked up her legs when she moved them.

She mustn't fall.

Her feet touched the floor. By pushing on the bed with her clenched fists she managed to raise herself; apart from one dreadful moment when she thought she was going to slip, there was nothing very hard about it. Her legs were stiff, and hurt a little when she moved. She stood by the bed, leaning on it to keep her balance, until she felt ready to move, then took a tiny jump forward. All the time she was expecting to hear the sound of footsteps on the stairs, and there was an almost overwhelming urge to rush things. She fought against it, realizing that if she did, she would most likely wreck her chances of getting out.

She neared the window.

Soon she was standing in front of it.

She could see a number of gardens. There was no one in any of them, although lines of washing hung out, blowing in the breeze, and from somewhere she could hear the rattle of a dustbin lid. If only it had been summer, she thought, there would have been at least one person sitting in the garden, whose attention she could have attracted.

Turning so that her back was to the wall, she leaned on it and worked her way down, until she was sitting with her back against the wall. She carried on until she was lying on the floor, then, as quickly as she dared, she rolled over until she was lying facing the window. From where she was now, the glass looked to be much too high off the ground for her to reach, and she felt a momentary panic. The hard floor hurt her wrists too, but there was nothing she could do about that.

She raised her legs until they were level with the glass.

Drawing them back, she kicked out as hard as she could. Both feet went through; there was a sharp pain as if she had cut herself, and the sound of glass falling into the yard below. That was something she would have to chance; whether Baggott and Madge would hear the noise and if they did, whether they would connect it with her.

She drew her feet back again. She could see blood on one of her stockings, but was relieved to see that it was only a small cut, although it bled freely, because of the sharp edges.

A jagged bit of glass stood up in the frame; it would make an excellent knife.

She began to move again, intending to

get where she could bring her bound wrists against it.

As she did so she heard the sound of footsteps on the stairs, and terror seized her as she realized that Baggott must be coming for her.

19

To her surprise the door opened very slowly and quietly. At first she thought that no one was coming in, and that they were merely looking to see that she was still there, but then she heard a sound.

The American came in.

He was alone.

He kept his eyes fixed on the bed, where she had been and where there was still a depression in the clothes, and then turned slowly, looking round the room. He saw her, and she knew that her eyes were widening with fear as he came across to her.

She whimpered.

He put a finger to his lips. 'Quiet, honey. I guess it's time that you and Tex hightailed outa here.'

She saw that he had a long gash on the side of his head, and that his hands were bloodstained from rubbing it. He bent down, and took out the knife that he had shown her before. Swiftly he cut the cords that bound her, and the familiar pains of cramp began again. When she was able to, she reached up and took off the gag.

Tex said: 'I'm sorry I can't offer you a drink. I guess I'm lucky to be here at all.' He rubbed a hand over his face wearily.

'You're taking me away from here?' she whispered.

'That's right, honey.' There was a touch of the old hardness in his voice. 'And in return, you're going to tell me where Bocking is, huh?'

Barbara opened her mouth. She was about to say that she had no idea where Tim was, but realized just in time that if she did so, and the American realized that she was telling the truth, not only would he not take her away, he might even kill her. If she kept up the pretence, there was just a chance that she would be able to get away, and certainly things couldn't be any worse than they were now.

She nodded.

He reached out his hand; she caught sight of the bloodstains again, and an explanation came to mind.

'Where's Baggott?'

The American laughed. 'Baggott's all right.' He saw what she was looking at and laughed again, softly. 'Don't worry, honey, I haven't killed anyone. Don't see any reason to kill you, either, only Baggott says so, but I guess that I'm not taking orders from him any more. Not after what he's done.'

'What has he done?'

Tex looked at his watch. 'I don't know if we should be standing here talking,' he muttered. 'Oh, hell, why worry?' He sat down on the edge of the bed. 'There'll be enough warning if anyone comes.'

'Oh, yes,' she said eagerly, 'there's a board that creaks, and — '

'I know.' A pause. 'Baggott tried to kill me.' The words came out flatly. 'To kill me,' he repeated.

'Why?' In spite of her fear Barbara was more than a little curious.

'So that he could deal with this on his own. It makes him about fifteen thousand pounds richer if I'm dead, and I guess that's a good enough motive. He must have thought it was a great idea to try to run me off the road, but he reckoned without my driving.'

He ran his hand lightly over the scratch on his face.

'I was going to shoot him up, but it seemed a better idea to take you and get the stuff from him.'

Only just in time she stopped herself from asking, what stuff? realizing that if she was supposed to know where Tim was she might be expected to know about this, too.

'Yeah, and save you! I never did want to kill you, but there was no reason before why I should fall out with Baggott about you. There is now. Let's go.' He stood up.

Almost without thinking, Barbara followed him to the door. He opened it, glanced out cautiously, then said: 'Follow me and don't make a sound if you want to come out of this alive.'

He had been so convincing in his assertion that he wouldn't kill her that she almost believed him. She followed him down the stairs; he stepped carefully on each board until he was certain that it wasn't going to creak. Once, he missed a step, and told her to do the same. Finally, they reached the bottom.

On their right was the front door.

On the left was a door that could only lead into the front room.

'Careful,' whispered the American, 'they can see the front door from the window.'

Reaching out cautiously, he began to turn back the catch on the front door, while Barbara stood just behind him, watching.

A hand clamped over her mouth without warning. A strong arm pulled her back, out of the way, then shoved her violently to one side. She saw Baggott. He was right behind the American, raising a gun. She fought violently, and managed to loosen the hand at her mouth slightly.

She screamed.

Tex whirled, just in time to avoid the downward blow that Baggott was smashing at him. With one arm he lashed out at the clown-like face, with the other he tried to grab the gun. Baggott swayed swiftly, then released Barbara, trying to smash the gun down.

Why didn't he shoot?

Barbara stood where she was, until she realized suddenly that the outcome of this fight *mattered* to her, and that if the American won there was a chance of freedom and safety. If Baggott won, there would only be pain and terror while he tried to make her tell what she didn't know.

She ran up behind Baggott, reaching up and grabbing his head, pulling as hard as she could. He tottered and the American moved in with a shout of triumph. Barbara pulled again. Her hand slipped. He wrenched himself free and raised his arm as the American hit out at him.

The hand with the gun in it!

He fired once.

Tex stopped, his arm still in the air. Slowly, the expression on his face changed to one of surprise, then he crashed to the ground, blood pouring from his head.

Barbara screamed again, Baggott turned, pushing her into the front room. 'I'm just about sick of this,' he snarled at her. 'It's time I got to work on you properly.'

Barbara stumbled over a small mat placed just inside the door. In the room she saw Madge, sitting in an armchair, twisted round to face them.

'What — ' she began as Baggott came in.

'Tex,' he told her briefly. 'Trying to get away with the kid. I had to shoot him.'

The woman showed no emotion. She stood up, took Barbara's shoulders and forced her into one of the other armchairs in the room.

'We'll see what she can tell us about Bocking,' she said.

Barbara looked up at her. Something about the cold, final way in which these people were speaking now, terrified her, and made her realize that unless she convinced them now that she knew nothing of what they wanted they would hurt her, and go on hurting her until they were convinced. She kept seeing the American, too, and the way he had crumpled up without a sound, dead.

Her mind seemed paralysed.

She said: 'Please — '

'Please nothing!' Baggott snapped. 'Where's Bocking?'

'I don't know!' She still couldn't think after what had happened. All she could do as he came nearer was to repeat: 'I don't know! I don't know!'

Madge said: 'You'll be glad to tell us when we start on you.'

'Stand up,' Baggott ordered. He still had the gun, which he was holding like a club, very near her head.

She didn't move.

'Stand up!' This time he roared at her, so that the words were just a blast of sound against her ears. Hardly knowing what she was doing, she stood up, leaning against the chair to stop herself from falling over.

Baggott was speaking more softly now, so that she could take in his meaning.

'Know how they used to question spies during the war? Know how they used to put them at a disadvantage, huh?'

He put his face very close to hers.

She shook her head.

'They used to make them strip before

251

they were questioned. The same applies to you now.'

She stepped back, but he moved too quickly for her, gripping her arms just above the elbows and lifting her off her feet. She struggled as he carried her over to Madge, but her blows had no effect on him at all. She felt the woman tugging at the zip of her dress, and screamed out.

'I've no idea where he is!'

Madge pulled the fastener down, and Baggott jerked her roughly back and forth. Her head whirled, until she didn't know what was happening, until Baggott gave her a sudden hard push that sent her staggering, until she fell.

'I don't know where he is,' she sobbed, trying to hold the dress up to her throat. 'I've no idea where he is!'

In the silence that followed a voice said softly: 'Ever thought that she might be right, Ray?'

It was the voice of Tim Bocking.

20

Barbara said: 'Tim, please help me.'

She was still on the floor, the dress falling off one shoulder.

He said: 'Shut up,' and turned away from her, to face Baggott and Madge. They remained still under the threat of the gun in his hand, Madge with her face expressionless, Baggott with compressed lips and glittering eyes.

Tim said: 'Barbara, get over there with the rest.'

Still wondering if she could make another chance to escape, she came over slowly and shakily.

'Why have you come here, Bocking?' Baggott growled.

'Why do you think? I've come to kill you.' His voice was remarkably calm, Barbara thought.

'Why?' Madge almost whispered.

'Why do you think? You three are the only ones who can say what part I played in this racket. If I shut you up, no one can prove a thing.'

Madge said slowly, painfully: 'You killed Johnny, didn't you?'

Tim nodded. 'He knew too much. I'll tell you something else, Madge, just to show how serious I am about this. While I was at the window waiting for a chance to get Johnny, Clare Roberts raised the sunblind. She saw me, and the little fool came out after me. I had to do something or she would have blown the whole thing.'

'She's dead too?' Baggott queried.

'I let her come to my flat,' Bocking answered.

Barbara opened her mouth to say something, then shut it again, appalled by all this killing. So Tim was just as bad as the rest, worse, in fact.

'I've got to kill you all,' he was saying slowly. 'I've already had a go at Tex but he got away. You did a much better job, didn't you, Ray?'

'He was trying to double-cross me.' Baggott's voice was surly. 'He was trying to take the girl.'

'Was he? Are you sure that he didn't

think my attempt to kill him was something arranged by you, and he wanted to get his own back?' He turned to Barbara. 'And why are you in all this?'

'Because she knew where you were,' Madge answered.

'What made you think that?'

'Clare Roberts told us.'

Bocking laughed shortly. 'Go on.'

'When you vanished we went to Clare, seeing as she was your girlfriend, and asked her if she knew where you were. She didn't, that was plain, but she told us that you'd been knocking around with this Barbara Young and that it must have been part of something you'd fixed up with her. So, we got Babs.'

'Very clever of Clare,' Bocking sneered. 'She was as jealous as hell about Barbara, you know. I think she'd have done anything to get rid of her.'

He paused.

'Listen, Baggott, the only reason either of them came into it was because I had to have someone at Lennon's to cover up the frauds from that angle. Clare Roberts, as Johnny's secretary, was ideal, but when we had that row I knew I couldn't trust her, so I ditched her and started on Barbara. Ever since then, Clare has been chasing me around. She's just jealous, trying to get her own back on Babs for pinching her boyfriend.'

He laughed, looking at Barbara.

'Pity she's signed your death warrant by doing it.'

His eyes went slowly over the small group and then came back to the girl.

'Yes,' he repeated. 'I wanted to use you to cover my tracks at Lennon's by getting hold of some of the books for me. I hadn't known you for long before I realized that you wouldn't do things like that, but by then it was too late to go back, so I've had to take a chance there. Everything else is prepared, I've an alibi ready and apart from those books there's only you lot can prove anything against me. I'll have to kill you.'

He swung the gun on to Madge.

'Starting with you.'

She screamed. Before he had time to fire Baggott had taken advantage of the fact that the weapon was away from him.

He leapt forward, covering the distance between him and Bocking in one stride and knocking his gun arm up so that the gun went off, plaster showering down from the ceiling. It rained down on Barbara, making her cough and choke as it caught in her throat. Her eyes streamed; when she could see properly again, Baggott and Tim were on the floor, Baggott on top, while Madge hovered near them, trying to get in a blow with her shoe but fearful of hitting Baggott.

Barbara started towards the door.

As she did so, Tim managed to get his arm out from under his body, holding the gun. He brought it down on the side of Baggott's head until the man loosened his hold and fell forward, so that Tim could scramble out from beneath him.

Madge ran forward.

Tim grabbed her as she ran, swung her round and pushed her back across the room. She cannoned into Barbara and the two women staggered, until Madge slipped and fell, bringing Barbara down with her.

Baggott lay still, one side of his head

sticky with blood. Madge also lay without moving, her head against the table leg that had knocked her unconscious.

Tim said: 'That only leaves you, doesn't it, Barbara?'

He came nearer. She screamed, more terrified by the set smile on his face than his threats. As he reached out for her she put up both hands to ward him off, but it was a weak, useless gesture and he brushed it aside effortlessly.

She knew he would have to kill her to be safe.

After all, she knew almost as much as Baggott and Madge. The only thing she didn't know was what the racket had been that they were involved in; all she knew about that was that its profits had been huge.

Tim was very close now.

She tried to scream again, but no sound came.

His fingers clamped round her neck and began to squeeze.

★ ★ ★

258

The more she struggled to try and throw him off, the more his fingers seemed to tighten round her throat. Her struggles became weaker, until they almost stopped. She knew that her eyes and mouth were wide open, and that her tongue was protruding, but that was all. That, and the great pain in her chest and the savage roaring in her ears blotted out everything else.

Soon, she knew nothing.

★   ★   ★

At about the same time as Barbara was eating from the tray that Madge Little had brought her, her father was walking past the Community Centre. He had stayed at Lennon's as long as he reasonably thought he could, and then walked slowly towards home, leaving his car where he had parked it. The murder, which had been so near to him, seemed to have numbed his mind, so that he couldn't think. As he walked he bumped into people, some of whom turned to stare at him, but he ignored them. It was almost mid-day now, and he could easily reach home in time to make himself a meal, but somehow the thought of preparing one himself and eating it alone was unappealing.

He saw a café and went in.

It was crowded with workers, but he managed to find one seat left at a four-seater table, and sat down, sharing the table with three teenage girls who talked noisily about pop singers while they ate, reminding him of Barbara, and of the way she had stuck pictures on the wall of her bedroom not long ago, and then been upset when he had to take them down in order to decorate.

He finished the meal quickly and left.

The next thing was to get something for Millie. All the time he had been at the hospital he had been conscious of the fact that he had brought nothing with him, and he had resolved to get something, some flowers or some fruit, or both, as soon as he got the chance, and to take them to Millie that evening. As he walked he tried to remember the bit of information that Coates wanted.

Where did Bocking work?

He had heard Barbara mention it, he was sure, but there had been no more reason to take particular notice of that than there had been to remember any of the other bits of information she had given about him. They had seemed to add up to someone to whom Harry could trust his daughter, and that was all that mattered.

Now, the name was important, for some reason that he didn't know.

It refused to come back to him.

He crossed the road and headed towards the Market Hall. There were flower shops round there, and lots of other shops where he might buy something that Millie would like. He knew that nothing he did would take her mind off Barbara, but he might be able to help for a short time.

When he reached the Hall itself he didn't go in, as at this time of the day there would be too many crowds there for his liking, and in any case he didn't like to buy at Market Stalls, always connecting them with cheap, shoddy goods.

He saw a shop, a kind of supermarket, where he could get what he wanted, and went in.

They sold flowers here; they were stacked all round one part of the shop, neatly tied in bundles and priced. He chose a bunch, and carried it over to the cash desk, surprised that he had been able to get such a good choice at this time of the year. Chocolates were cunningly placed in large stands by the desk, so that customers had to stand by them while they were queuing to pay, and were almost certain to pop one of the blocks into their bags.

He stepped past two women who were waiting there, and chose a large box of chocolates before joining the short queue.

The girl's fingers flew up and down the buttons on the cash register, so that Harry's turn came much more quickly than he had expected. Feeling slightly sheepish he handed over the flowers. The girl took them with a smile, wrapped a sheet of tissue paper round them with a deft twist of her hand, and handed them back. The chocolates went into a brown paper bag.

'Twenty-three shillings altogether,' the girl said, still smiling at him.

He handed over the money, took his change, and caught sight of a badge pinned to her pale pink overall.

The mental block in his mind seemed to clear suddenly. Goodfare Supermarket. He stood on the pavement for a moment, then turned and almost ran.

Goodfare Supermarket.

That was where Bocking had worked, only not in the shop itself but in the offices. He went to phone Superintendent Coates.

21

Coates arrived at the main offices of the Goodfare Supermarket about half an hour later, alone in the police car, but with a second car alerted and on its way. Sergeant Hopkins was still with the Divisional men at Bocking's flat, searching for anything that might help in the murder of Clare Roberts.

Certainly Bocking was urgently wanted now.

Why hadn't the Goodfare people come forward before with any information that they had?

The office itself was on the first floor of one of the older office blocks near Waterloo, and from it was controlled the chain of shops which covered the whole of the outer London area.

Coates went into the Enquiry office, and held a short conversation with a girl there, who blinked absurdly long eyelashes at him and told him that she wouldn't be a moment. Five minutes later she came back and showed him into the office of the manager.

'Good afternoon, Mr. Goodman,' Coates began. 'I understand that you have an employee named Bocking. Is this correct?'

Goodman, a large man almost as tall as the policeman, stood up.

'I'm afraid it is,' he said heavily. 'Such a bright young man, too. I've only just found out myself that he was wanted by the police. I was going to call you right away.'

'Were you?'

'Of course.' Goodman looked surprised.

'How did you find out we wanted him?'

'From the radio. There was an annoucement.'

'There have been announcements all morning, Mr. Goodman,' Coates answered, 'and I'm surprised that in an organization like this you haven't heard before. How long had Bocking been missing from work?'

'Not as long as it may seem, actually. He was away a week on a course, you know, and then he never turned up after that. We thought that something had detained him there and expected him to ring us but he never did.' He smiled faintly. 'I can see why now.'

'I see.' Coates glanced round the office. 'What did he do here?'

'He was an accountancy trainee. Very good, too, extremely bright.'

'Was he?' A tiny suspicion flashed at the back of the superintendent's mind. 'Who actually owns this firm?' He managed to make the question appear very casual.

'Who owns — ' Goodman began.

'You know what I mean, Mr. Goodman. You don't own it yourself, do you?'

'No, but — '

'Then who does?'

Goodman spread his hands, as if acknowledging some kind of defeat. 'A Miss Little, Miss Madge Little,' he said.

* * *

Coates broke the silence that followed.

'What's the racket, Mr. Goodman?'

'Racket? I'm afraid I don't quite follow

266

you, Mr. Coates.'

'Then I'll piece together the case as far as I've got it,' Coates said. 'The manager of a large firm of tobacco wholesalers was shot dead this morning. His sister owns this chain of shops. One of your workers has disappeared, and his ex-girlfriend has been murdered in his flat. There are other things which I'm not going to go into, but to me they all add up to a racket. It seems to me, too, that you've kept very quiet about employing Bocking, and that must mean you're involved.'

'Are you accusing me, Superintendent?' Goodman's face was white.

'I can do nothing officially while I'm here on my own, but you'd be advised to tell me everything you know.'

There was a silence then Goodman seemed to crumple. He went behind his desk and sat for a moment with his hands flat on the desk top, then, slowly, the story came out.

The racket had been run, he said, by two men, an American whose name he didn't know, and a man called Baggott, who also used the alias Jenkins. Originally, they had bribed men at Lennon's warehouse to put the wrong labels on a few boxes a week while they were loading, so that the goods came into their hands. When Little had come to work there it hadn't taken him long to find out what was going on, but instead of reporting it he had tried to be clever and find out who was behind it. Eventually the gang had frightened him so much that he was forced to work for them.

Now, they had the opportunity to expand.

Instead of merely taking a few boxes a week, they could get him to use his greater authority, and misdirect whole lorry loads. The only trouble with this was that they soon began to find it difficult to get rid of so many goods regularly.

They had found out that Madge Little owned this chain of shops.

She had been forced into the racket, although from what Goodman had heard she had needed very little persuasion. She had forced him to work with her, and all had gone well until Bocking had spotted various false entries in the books, and had demanded a cut in the profits as his price for keeping quiet. Plans were made for killing him, but he had vanished — taking with him thirty thousand pounds of the gang's money.

That was all Goodman knew.

He sat silently in his chair while Coates called for the patrol car, charged him and had him taken away.

★   ★   ★

Coates and a constable went in Coates' car to Madge Little's house. Leaving the constable by the gate, the superintendent knocked loudly on the front door. There was no reply; with a sick feeling that he was too late he stepped back, glancing up at the windows.

He saw nothing.

He went along the path at the front of the house, until he could see in through the front windows.

He saw a man, his hands fastened tightly round a young girl's neck.

Without thought of his own danger, he smashed the window with one blow. The man looked up, letting the girl fall heavily to the floor, obviously unconscious.

Coates said: 'Police. Stay where you are.'

He smashed out more of the glass, and heard the sound of a siren as a patrol car drew up outside the gate. The man turned and ran swiftly out of the room. Coates climbed in at the window. Men came running up the path. Coates slipped round to the front door, seeing the body sprawled by it, and opened it.

Five constables came in.

'Get round the house, outside,' he ordered. 'One of you have a look at the girl.'

He turned and started up the stairs. He had heard the noise of Bocking's feet as he had ran up here, but now everything was silent. Aware that the fugitive probably had a gun, Coates went slowly, keeping well to one side, where he could see all the doors which opened off the landing.

Only one was ajar.

One of the constables shouted: 'He might have a gun, sir!' and ran up the stairs after him.

They heard the sound of breaking glass. As Coates started forward, the constable put out a refraining hand.

'Let me go in first, sir.'

'Don't worry about me!' Coates snapped. 'It's Bocking we want.'

When they got into the room, Bocking was half out of the window, one foot on a ladder. He saw the policemen come in, and glanced down, then scrambled hastily as the constable rushed forward.

Too hastily.

His feet slipped.

Coates heard a faint murmur of sound from the men outside as Bocking plunged downwards.

★　★　★

'How's the girl?'

'Not too bad, sir.' The lounge seemed

271

full of policemen. 'They've taken her to hospital in one ambulance and the rest of them in another. The chap in the hall was dead, but the others may live.'

Coates said: 'It's the girl I'm bothered about.'

*   ★   *

At the hospital, a young, fresh-faced doctor, leaned over the still unconscious Barbara. This was John Benson, called as the girl had been a patient of Maurice Franklin, and was now technically one of his patients. He flushed slightly when he recognized the girl from the photos that the police had shown him, then turned his attention to her breathing and the ugly marks on her throat.

At length he completed his examination, and straightened up.

'She'll be all right,' he said softly to Harry Young who was sitting nearby. 'All she needs is a lot of care and attention.'

The look in his eyes told Harry that he intended to make sure she got it, too.

We do hope that you have enjoyed reading this large print book.

Did you know that all of our titles are available for purchase?

We publish a wide range of high quality large print books including:
Romances, Mysteries, Classics
General Fiction
Non Fiction and Westerns

Special interest titles available in large print are:
The Little Oxford Dictionary
Music Book, Song Book
Hymn Book, Service Book

Also available from us courtesy of Oxford University Press:
Young Readers' Dictionary
(large print edition)
Young Readers' Thesaurus
(large print edition)

For further information or a free brochure, please contact us at:
Ulverscroft Large Print Books Ltd.,
The Green, Bradgate Road, Anstey,
Leicester, LE7 7FU, England.
Tel: (00 44) **0116 236 4325**
Fax: (00 44) **0116 234 0205**

Other titles in the
Linford Mystery Library:

DEATH CALLED AT NIGHT

R. A. Bennett

Jimmy Ellis believes his parents have died in a car crash when as a young boy he is taken to live with relatives in Australia. The years pass happily, then the nightmare comes. Terrifying images flit through his mind in the dark — all through the eyes of a child, a witness to grisly events seventeen years before. He begins to delve into the past, and soon he finds himself on the trail of a double murderer — a murderer who is prepared to kill again.